PENGUIN BOOKS

Prayers of a Very Wise Child

Over the last twenty-five years Roch Carrier has written some of the most beloved books to come out of Quebec, including such classics as *La Guerre, Yes Sir!* and the abiding children's favourite, *The Hockey Sweater*. He continues to be read in both his original French and in English translation. Carrier's varied and expansive career has also steered him into the worlds of film, journalism and fine art—he wrote the text for *Canada Je T'aime/ I Love You*, a collaboration with painter Miyuki Tanoube. Carrier's novel, *Heartbreaks Along the Road*, was reissued by Penguin in 1991, and his most recent novel, *The Man in the Closet*, will be published by Penguin in 1993.

Sheila Fischman, the Governor General's award-winning translator, has created another graceful translation with *Prayers of a Very Wise Child*, her tenth Carrier title.

PRAYERS OF
A VERY WISE CHILD

Translated by Sheila Fischman

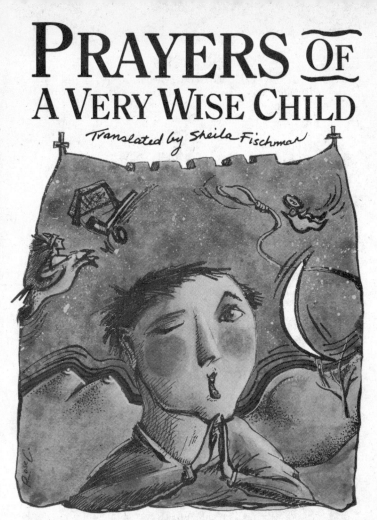

ROCH CARRIER

Author of The Hockey Sweater

Penguin Books

PENGUIN BOOKS
Published by the Penguin Group
Penguin Books Canada Ltd, 10 Alcorn Avenue, Toronto,
Ontario, Canada M4V 3B2
Penguin Books Ltd, 27 Wrights Lane, London W8 5TZ,
England
Penguin Books USA Inc., 375 Hudson Street, New York,
New York 10014, U.S.A.
Penguin Books Australia Ltd, Ringwood, Victoria, Australia
Penguin Books (NZ) Ltd, 182-190 Wairau Road,
Auckland 10, New Zealand

Penguin Books Ltd, Registered Offices:
Harmondsworth, Middlesex, England

First published in Viking by Penguin Books Canada Limited, 1991

Published in Penguin Books, 1992

1 3 5 7 9 10 8 6 4 2

Book design by Rose Cowles

*Publisher's note: This book is a work of fiction. Names, characters,
places and incidents either are the product of the author's
imagination or are used fictitiously, and any resemblance to actual
persons living or dead, events, or locales is entirely coincidental.*

Manufactured in Canada

Canadian Cataloguing in Publication Data
Carrier, Roch, 1937 –
[Prières d'un enfant très très sage. English]
Prayers of a very wise child
Translation of: Prières d'un enfant très très sage.
ISBN 0–14–014916–3
I. Title. II. Title: Prières d'un enfant très très sage. English.
PS8505.A77P713 1992   C843'.54   C91–094173–4
PQ3919.2.C37P713 1991

Introduction

Once there was a little boy who was born in the late 1930s. A world war broke out shortly after his birth. It wasn't his fault.

The world was complicated.

The little boy used to ask questions. Often the adults didn't know the answers, and that bothered them. To make it seem as if they *did* know, they sometimes made up fanciful answers. Other times, they thought the little boy was too young to understand the real answer, and then their responses were even more fanciful.

The little boy felt very much alone. Fortunately, God, who is everywhere, listened to his questions. Unfortunately, however, He didn't take the trouble to answer a little boy who wanted to know everything.

Today, God is still just as silent, and the little boy has become a man who remembers.

It wasn't the little boy's fault that the world was the way it was.

R.C.

Translator's Note

The "wise child" of the title was, to be quite accurate — and ironic — a very good little boy, a paragon of excellent behaviour. We might have evoked his true nature by referring in the English title to his sins as well as his prayers, but those who first encountered the boy and his dilemmas considered him to be already so gifted with wisdom that no other word would do him justice. I hope you enjoy this wise — and good, and wicked — little boy.

S.F.

Contents

1

Fire
Prayer

I came to talk to You here in Your church because You can hear me better. They say that in the cities there are buildings higher than the church steeple. That means You can't hear prayers so well in the cities, God. It's why they have such terrible problems in the cities. In our village the houses have just two storeys and an attic. Sometimes when the grown-ups go upstairs they have to duck their heads to keep from bumping into the ceiling. The church is ten times bigger than the houses. Oh, way more than ten even: thirty-nine or forty-seven times bigger. The point of the steeple sticks into the sky. So when there's nobody in the church I talk out loud and You, God, up in Your Heaven, You stick Your ear against the point of our steeple as if it was a telephone, and You listen to me.

I really like to say little prayers in a whisper, but if You've been up in Heaven since the beginning of time I guess You must be the oldest person in the world. And if You're like the old people I know, You're probably going deaf. I'd rather talk out loud, then, so You can hear me, with Your ear up against the church steeple the way I press my ear to a glass against the wall, to find out what our sisters are whispering in their bedroom.

This church is the new church. Because the other one, the old one, burned down. Our parents say the fire in the old church happened two years before I was born. But I remember that fire very well. If I wasn't born yet, God, why is it I remember that fire in the church so well? Our mother sent me to the dictionary to look up all the different meanings of the verb "to lie." Is remembering lying?

I can still hear the wood crackling. I can still see the smoke rising. I can see the flames spilling out of the windows, and flowing like lava. The church was like a volcano. It roared! It was burning like a log in the stove. The flames were as high as a

mountain, an angry red mountain. I'll never forget the sound of the explosion when the fire burst
through the roof. I saw chunks of the roof flying
over the village like fiery birds. I saw the steeple
tilt first to one side, then the other. It swayed, it
straightened up, it leaned over, and then it landed
on the ground like slow lightning. The devil
grabbed hold of Your house, God. He was spitting
blazing sparks at You in Heaven.

Even though I wasn't born until two years later,
I saw the old curé walk around the church and
sprinkle holy water on it. The children were
crying, the women were praying. The men had
formed a chain to haul buckets of water. So You
can see that I remember, can't You God?

I've never seen the ocean. One day I will. The
fire was like terrifying waves. All at once, the wind
was blowing harder. The ocean was heading
straight for our village. I remember very well, we
were living in the big brick house across the street
from the church. Our mother was holding me in
her arms, against her chest. When she saw the
flames racing towards us, our mother got scared.

She held me really tight, as if she was clinging to me. Our house was trembling. The earth was shaken by that ocean of fire. I couldn't help our mother: I was too little. According to her, I wasn't even born yet.

God, I saw the skeleton of the church traced in red against the night, as if it was black paper.

I saw everything I'm telling You, just like I'm telling it. The proof that I saw the old church in the village burn down, God, is that I'm telling You how it burned.

I'm not lying either. I'm just telling what I know. And I've told You what I remember. I can't help it if You gave me a good memory. Our mother says I remember the fire in the old church better than she does.

Thank You, God, for putting such an excellent memory in my child's body. I came to tell You, I promise I'll never forget that definition of the verb "to lie" our mother made me look up in the dictionary.

And I also promise, God, to live a full life so I'll have lots of memories to remember. Thank You for giving us a beautiful new church where I can pray to You.

Please God, give a memory to those who don't have one. I'm going out to play hockey now. That's why I'm wearing my skates. Because I forgot to take them off. Amen.

2

Moon Prayer

Today, God, I'm going to pray in my bed instead of going to the church. Thank You for the beautiful day You gave the Earth. I caught three big trouts in the Famine River, but I threw back a big carp. God, Your carp are really poor quality. They can't take the summer heat. Their flesh decomposes as if they were dead. But anyway, the bees and the butterflies seemed to be happy about everything. The day passed as quickly as the night does when you're asleep. I picked some strawberries, too. I brought home my trouts and a pailful of strawberries, already hulled. I'm not the kind of lazybones that picks strawberries and then doesn't hull them. But I think You could have made strawberries that don't have hulls. They'd be easier to pick.

Our mother sent me out to cord some wood. It's

the beginning of July, and the sun's so hot you melt in your pants. But our father's getting ready for the winter. He's bought his wood, enough to heat every igloo at the North Pole and the polar ice cap, too. And we're the ones that have to cord it. Summer holidays would be the best time in my whole life if it wasn't for cording that wood. Sometimes when I look at the mountain of wood waiting for me, I wonder if I wouldn't be better off in school, learning lists of grammatical exceptions and how to make fishes plural.

It was really beautiful today. You should have seen Your sun, and the colour of the barley and the spruce trees. You should have heard Your birds singing and Your insects buzzing. You should have seen Your snakes baking their skins on piles of stones: You'd have been proud of Yourself. Days like that mean that the eternal goodness of Your Heaven overflowed onto Earth. I want to thank You, God, for the beautiful day. Even if tears are pouring out of my eyes, I'm really quite happy. It's dark in my room but You can see me. The tears are on account of our Uncle Marcel.

You're the only one that knows I'm bawling like a baby. When I cry I don't make any sound, I don't sniff or squawk. I suffer my sorrow in silence, as they say on the radio. If my brothers hear me crying they'll make fun of me and call me a baby. One sob and they'll be in my bed, landing on me with their feet and slapping me with their pillows. I'd rather keep my suffering inside for a while. My pillow's all wet. I really shouldn't be suffering like this after such a beautiful day.

Our Uncle Marcel is young and he's taller than me. He must be at least thirteen or twelve, our uncle. He's the one that holds the censer in the church procession. If you ask me, I think he'd rather be holding some girl's hand. Uncle Marcel smokes on the sly. That's a secret, but I can tell You because You've seen him. His mother, our grandmother, doesn't know. I think I'll tell her tomorrow. Uncle Marcel upset me a lot tonight. I know he smokes because he offered me his cigarette and he said:

"If you don't tell my mother, your grandmother, I'll let you take a puff."

I didn't take one puff, I took a dozen. All at once I felt like a man: I was dizzy and I wanted to throw up. My guts were squirming, my head was spinning. I still didn't say anything to Uncle Marcel's mother, our grandmother. Tomorrow, if You let me live long enough to open my eyes, I'm going to tell our grandmother on him because he upset me so much. I can't stand it when people laugh at me because I'm not as big as the others and because I'm younger.

Our Uncle Marcel is proud. He's always got a little mirror in one hand, and with the other hand he's always combing his hair. He wants the girls to think he's handsome. I'm going to tell our grandmother that he made me smoke. Then Uncle Marcel will be sentenced to stay in his room for quite a few nights. He'll have to go quite a few days without combing his hair because he'll have to go quite a few days without any girls seeing him. My pillow's all wet with tears, God, and I don't like going to sleep feeling sad.

Tonight our father said:

"The Moon's as full as a woman."

I didn't understand what he meant. I looked at the Moon. She was like a great big orange on a tablecloth, as blue as the sky, that had little holes like moth-holes in it, for the stars. The Moon also looked like the big round head of a man, without any hair or a toupee or a body, but with eyes and a nose and a mouth. If the Moon was full, she was full of light. And I was looking up at her.

I wished I could reach up and touch Your Moon. I wished I could climb onto the Moon and scoop up a handful, like a handful of earth or a handful of snow. I wished I could see what it was made of. Is the Moon a ball of fire? Is the Moon just an explosion? Is the Moon solid like Earth? Is it a big diamond? Is it like a huge scoop of ice cream you can lick? Is it hot like fire? Is it cold like ice? Anyway, it's beautiful to look at. It's so far away from Earth that looking at it for a long time makes you dizzy, like when Uncle Marcel made me smoke a string cigarette. Our Uncle Marcel hasn't got any tobacco. He won't steal any from his father, our grandfather, because he says he's not a thief, so I bring him string from our father's store.

God, You hung the Moon so high up in the sky, it would take four hundred years to get there by train. That's what the nun at school told us. She didn't say how long it would take to build the railway. You'd have to know how long it took to build the railway that goes from one end of Canada to the other. And then calculate the distance between Earth and the Moon. Then divide that distance by the length of Canada. And then multiply the quotient obtained by the time needed to build the Canadian railway. The Moon's far, far away, farther than the end of our lives.

Nobody on the gallery outside our house dared to talk. We were all looking at the Moon. We were as quiet as if we were scared. It was a nice kind of fear, though. A gentle fear. The sleepy kind of fear when you don't understand something beautiful that you wish you could understand. It was as if the gallery had moved like a boat in the water. The men were smoking. The women were quiet, too. You could hear yourself breathe. That was the only sound our lives were making. The Moon was beautiful, round and yellow and shiny. There were a few stars, but you just knew that on this night, the sky was made for the Moon. It was really hard to believe that some of the stars were hundreds of times bigger than the Moon: they seemed to be hundreds of times smaller. The Moon was the queen of the stars, I tell You. Maybe the Moon isn't a star because it doesn't have points like a real star, but anyway, she was really shiny and far away up in the sky where the stars are, and where You are too, God. The sky You created on the first day of Creation is very beautiful; I wonder if it's become more beautiful since. You created it perfect, but if it's more beautiful now, it's Your fault. Thank You for beauty, God.

There were quite a lot of us out on the gallery. The men didn't dare to smoke. The children were quiet. We felt as if we weren't exactly on the Earth: as if we'd floated a little on our gallery, between Earth and the Moon. And it felt as if Earth was flying in the sky.

There was practically a crowd of us out on the gallery: Monsieur Philippe from the elections and Roméo the ice-cream man and Juste and Madame

Juste and Roland and Réal and Gaston who make heels for ladies' shoes; there was Dorval who sells horses and all my brothers and sisters and the seminary student who's learning to read from a breviary and the thirteen Chabotte children. And then there were my friends Roger and Lapin. I'm pretty sure I've left out some but You saw them all, God, all sitting on the gallery and not talking.

Everybody was looking at the sky that had never been so bright. The sky was as blue as in the middle of the day. The sky above the village seemed as light as a curtain when the wind blows in. Behind the curtain, it was as if we could see You. It felt as if You were there. As we listened, it was as if we could hear You smoking Your pipe up in Heaven. But there wasn't any smoke: the sky was clean, without a cloud. In the cities, apparently, people never see the sky on account of the black clouds the factories make. I imagine people get out of the habit of looking at the sky, so they forget. Since people forget the things they don't see very often, they must forget You, too, God.

Our Uncle Marcel was sitting out on the gallery

too. He was quiet because if he'd said anything, our grandmother who was out there too, rocking, would have told him to go and make his noise somewhere else. He'd been quiet for a long time. Even though there weren't any girls to admire him, our Uncle Marcel's hair was combed better than anybody's; he looked really sharp. Uncle Marcel's the best player in any game; he's the fastest runner; he's got the worst temper. If there's girls around, it's Uncle Marcel they like best, and that makes me proud.

Our Uncle Marcel isn't one of those people who walks by you with his nose in the air so he can't smell you, as if you were a cat turd. He's practically twice as old as I am, but sometimes he plays with me as if he wasn't an uncle and he was the same age as me. Sometimes we even have fights. We roll in the grass like real enemies, but we laugh, and then we roll some more and we bang into each other and give each other wrist burns and we kick and rip each other's shirts and hit our heads on the grass and put our hands around each other's necks and choke, but we choke from laughing, too. Sometimes I cry because I'm smaller and because Uncle Marcel is better. But I'm proud of our uncle, even though I never win a fight with him. I don't know anybody else that's got an uncle who plays with him and rolls in the grass all the way from the road down to the vegetable garden. Everybody else with uncles has old uncles who are bald and scared they'll fall down and break their bones and kick a bucket. I'm really proud of our Uncle Marcel. Sometimes I try to comb my hair like him. When I'm grown up like him I'll be the best, like him, and I'll have the worst temper like him and I'll hit the ball as far as he does. The girls will know I'm the best.

Our Uncle Marcel was looking at the Moon, too, and he was quiet. But then all of a sudden he talked. Beside the house You planted a willow tree, an old, old one that was there long before the house. It's way higher than the house and its trunk is as wide as my bed. Four or five other trunks are growing out of the first one. Sitting on one of its branches is like climbing on the back of our father's horse.

The Earth had turned, or maybe the Moon had moved, and Uncle Marcel said in my ear, so he wouldn't interrupt the other people's thinking:

"See that? The Moon's in the willow tree."

I looked with the eyes You gave me, God, and I saw the Moon in the willow tree, just like Uncle Marcel said.

"See? The Moon's up there on the biggest branch of the willow."

He said this in a whisper, and he was pointing at the Moon. Some of the people sitting on the gallery looked where his finger was pointing.

"Look, up there, leaning against the tip of the biggest branch: it's the Moon."

I stood up to get a better look. It was true. Uncle Marcel had noticed before any of the others that the Moon had stopped; she'd landed on the biggest branch. The Moon was hooked onto the end of the biggest branch, way up high above the roof of the house, higher than the chimney, almost as high as the church steeple, practically at the top of the willow.

"Yes, you're right," I said to our Uncle Marcel, "I can see the Moon perched at the very end of the biggest branch."

This time he spoke out loud:

"Want me to go up and get you a couple of handfuls of moon?"

"Yes," I told him, "I want three handfuls of moon, or four."

Everybody on the gallery heard our uncle, and they heard me answer. Everybody watched our uncle get out of his chair, walk down off the gallery, go to the willow, jump up, and then, with his neatly combed hair and his nice clean clothes, start to climb that tree, as limber as a cat, without mussing his hair. Everybody was watching our uncle, especially that Clémence Chabotte who'd just arrived, she's the sister of Juste Chabotte's boys. I was really proud of our Uncle Marcel. I didn't know anybody else with an uncle like mine, that could climb a willow tree to bring down a handful of moon for his nephew. I stood up so I could watch him better. He was already high up; I could see the leaves stirring and tossing higher and higher. And then, all of a sudden, very high up, almost at the very end of the big branch, I saw our uncle right beside the Moon. I saw him touch the Moon. And then I saw him pull off a handful, two handfuls, three handfuls of moon; I saw him scoop up some moon the way you scoop up water in your hand. I was so happy! I was going to have some pieces of the Moon! I didn't know anybody else that had pieces of moon. I'd take them to show at school. No other uncle would dare to go up as high as our Uncle Marcel. I was proud, God, prouder than I'd ever been in my whole life.

Our uncle climbed back down as easily as he'd gone up. He came back to the gallery, slowly and carefully because he was carrying moon dust. It was fragile, I told myself. It could die and turn grey like ashes. It could scatter in the wind. Our Uncle Marcel was being careful. He was protecting his harvest. He was taking tiny little steps. He was hardly lifting his feet as he came towards us, with both hands closed around his catch that seemed to want to fly away like a bird. When he got really close to me, our Uncle Marcel said very loud:

"Still want a piece of moon?"

"Yes!"

I was so happy, I almost shouted.

Everybody came over quietly, like in church, to get a look at the piece of moon our Uncle Marcel had gone to get me in the sky, at the tip of the willow tree. He told me:

"Count to three. At three I'll open my hands . . ."

I was a little bit scared. I'd never touched moon before. Was it cold like ice? Was it hot like bread? I got my own hands ready to move fast.

He counted: "One, two . . . three . . ."

Our Uncle Marcel's hands were partly open and I caught the piece of moon. It was cool and wet. Everybody was looking at me. I was looking at the piece of moon. It wasn't shiny. It was wet. Crumpled. I looked more closely. It wasn't shiny. It wasn't ashes. It wasn't moon. It was a handful of leaves. So then I yelled:

"That isn't moon, it's willow leaves."

They all burst out laughing as if I'd made some funny joke. Everybody. Even our Uncle Marcel, who never laughs for fear of mussing his hair. Even Your seminary student. Even that Clémence Chabotte, who must think her Marcel's the best.

19

Moon
Prayer

I burst into tears like a bomb. Honest, God, I've never cried so hard in my whole life.

When I'm very old I'll still remember that Moon. It's so sad when grown-ups play tricks on you. I'm going to stop praying to You now, God, and I'm going to cry into my pillow because I still haven't cried out all my sorrow.

Roch
Carrier

3

Indians
Prayer

Do You hate the smell of fish, God? I'm sorry about stinking up Your church, but if I'd left my fish outside, the cats would have come and eaten them. . . . And if I'd left them in the water, I couldn't eat them tonight. I've got three trouts, pretty good-sized ones. They smell strong, but not as strong as a big sin I think.

The other night when I came back from the river I put five nice, shiny trouts on the kitchen table. Our mother was busy cutting up fudge into squares. There were enough trouts for the whole family, so she should've been happy with my catch, but instead she got annoyed.

"Take those animals off the table! I can't stand it! There's nothing more disgusting than fish."

I don't agree with that. God, Your fish are as beautiful as Your birds. When things are normal, our mother likes fish. She likes to show us the frying-pan with a row of trouts lying on their backs in butter and their pretty little bellies cut open and stuffed with herbs.

When our mother gets mad she isn't in a normal state. I've lived long enough now, God, I have an idea what's going on. When our brother arrived, I didn't understand a thing. When our sister came a year later, I wasn't surprised.

It starts off first of all with our mother being impatient. Not impatient like a mother bringing up children, the other kind: the impatience that comes with important events.

A little later, she complains about her dresses: they're too small. So then our father tells her there's nothing wrong with the dresses, she's just put on some weight. Our father isn't trying to be mean; he smiles when he says it, to tease her. Our mother, who's impatient in an abnormal way, gets mad. In the house it's like a storm, and sometimes dishes get broken. That's when our father decides to go outside. He takes his hat because it's a good idea for him to stay outside for quite a while. But our father knows that the storm is a sign of the important event.

Suddenly our mother buys new dresses. Now she can't complain that they're too small, so she says they're too hot for the summer. Our father turns very cautious.

"Pretty soon it'll be fall and it won't be so hot, and then, my dear, you'll be getting thin."

After our father says that he waits a while. Sometimes our mother smiles. If she doesn't smile, our father realizes he'd better take his hat off the hook and go outside. We just keep quiet. There's peace, but we can smell the danger very near.

After that comes fudge time. We're back from school and the whole house smells of fudge. If the wind is blowing properly you can smell the sugary smell from far away. Our mother's standing by the wood stove. She has a big spoon and she's stirring the fudge in a great big kettle. She watches the bubbles and the bubbles tell her what to do: add a pinch of sugar, stir it thirty-three more times, add a drop of water or run and stick the pot in cold water. We aren't allowed to taste. We're almost drowning in the perfume of sugar and cream: good sweet sugar, just a little burnt; our lips lick the smell of maple fudge. No, we mustn't touch. Mustn't even brush one finger against the squares of fudge lined up on the table. That's for AFTER. When I hear that now, God, I know the rest: the Indians are coming!

You know as well as I do, God, what happens when the Indians are coming closer. Our mother suddenly turns patient. We could dance on the lace tablecloth for special Sundays, and she wouldn't say a word. She smiles. She hands out smiles. We wonder why. She isn't supposed to smile. We haven't seen her smile for months.

Our father, though, he hasn't *stopped* smiling for months. Then all of a sudden he stops. He gets mad if you spill a glass of milk or come to the table just a bit late or if you shove our sister; he blows up. His tempers are a lot worse than our mother's. If You want to make really good hurricanes or typhoons or electrical storms, God, I recommend You take Your inspiration from our father's storms. The Indians are coming, you can tell.

It's always the same thing. We come home from school and we're told that we aren't allowed in the house. Our mother's getting ready for the arrival of the Indians. Old Laetitia's helping her. Both of them look pretty busy. I don't know what they're doing. Our father's never there. When the Indians get too close he always has to go to the far end of his territory at Saint-Magloire-de-Bellechasse on account of his business. Could it be that our father's afraid of the Indians?

I'd sure like to know what the Indians do to our mother. The only thing I ask You is to give me the time to grow up and find out. Some day, if it is Your will, I'll be big enough, and then, if our mother needs me to, I'll defend her, I promise You.

So then we have to go to our grandparents'. It's already time to go to the table. Our grandfather soaks his bread in maple syrup, with his fingers. Our grandmother tells him that's no kind of manners to teach children. And our grandfather gives her these little looks, his eyes all wrinkled with mischief.

"You're right, woman, I'll teach them how to eat their syrup with a fork and you can tell them what the Indians are doing to their mother."

Our grandmother turns as red as a raspberry.

"You're a wicked old man, and the older you get the wickeder you are!"

Our grandfather laughs. He's pleased with himself. He dips his bread in his syrup. Only he's forgotten to take a slice of bread, so his fingers get soaked. It's like that every time the Indians come to visit.

Then we have to go to bed. It's hard to sleep. We think about the Indians. We'd really like to know what they're doing to our mother. We never see the Indians. I don't know a single child who ever has. When you ask grown-ups about the Indians they give you answers that don't make much sense. They say they've never seen them either.

Apparently, the Indians beat our mothers. All the mothers in the village have been beaten by the Indians. If the Indians don't exist, from what I've heard in the general store, then tell me, God, who is it that beats our mothers really, really hard? They stay in bed for a whole week and sometimes longer. I can't understand why our fathers don't defend our mothers. They ought to get out their guns. If they don't want to declare war on the Indians, they ought to prevent them from getting in the house: bolt the door, seal the windows, plug the chimney. Why does our father run away to Saint-Magloire-de-Bellechasse when the Indians come?

When they leave again, after they've beaten our mother, the Indians always leave a squalling baby behind in the crib. It looks like a hairless rabbit squirming around in a snare. And it cries loud enough to break windows. Babies aren't a very good invention. They pee. Everybody has to take care of them. I'd rather be in a family that didn't have a squalling baby.

We think about all that in our bedroom at the grandparents'. It's a strange room. It's a bed we don't know. There's straw in the mattress that prickles your bum. We're worried about our mother. We don't like the Indians. We can't make them not leave a baby at the house. If the baby's a girl it's even worse. On the wall there's all kinds of scary shadows. You think. You shut your eyes, but you see more things than if you'd kept them open. You fall asleep in the middle of the night. And then you sleep like logs. And you don't realize you've wet the bed.

God, do You remember when You used to wet Your bed? . . . It's nothing to be proud of. Wetting the bed, at my age . . . it's the most shameful shame there is. In the morning, our grandfather's waiting for us with his mouthfuls of bread, his maple syrup and his little eyes all wrinkled with mischief.

"Grandmother," he says, "did you change our boy's diaper?"

"Stop teasing the little fellow. The urge to pee is one of God's laws and everybody obeys it, including the pope and the saints."

That morning, I knew the Indians had been at the house but I wasn't allowed to stop in and see on my way to school. Our grandmother said that maybe the Indians hadn't left yet. She went inside our house, though. She wasn't scared. But we had to go on to school. Walking past the house, looking at the windows, the door, and not knowing what's going on inside, not being able to go in and see, is like going away and never coming back. I cried.

When we got to the schoolyard everybody ran up to us.

"The Indians came to your house! The Indians came to your house!"

Everybody had heard the news. And everybody was laughing. The news must have been funny. Everybody seemed glad because the Indians had been at our house.

Big Red, You know him, he's the tallest boy, he's fourteen and he's got boots with iron around them like horseshoes, Big Red said to me:

"Your belly-button isn't dry yet, but I'm going to let you in on something: if the Indians beat your mother like they did mine last time, I warn you she'll be in bed for at least two novenas. After the Indians' visit our mother had broken legs and broken arms and both her eyes were black. Mother was knocked out so hard she couldn't even scold us. Her legs were broken in three places, her arms in four. And when the Indians went away they left behind three twins. Twins that don't even look the same: they're as different as you and me. Aside from that, the Indians wrung my mother's neck like a dishcloth."

Class started. We said our prayers to You. Then we listened to the catechism, and after that arithmetic and reading. I was only thinking about our mother. When would we see her again? Two novenas in bed was what Big Red had said. Who would cook the meat and wash the dishes and scrub the shirts and help us with our homework and do our laundry and sweep the house and darn our socks and wax the floor? I asked myself all those questions. Who'd take care of the baby? Maybe the Indians had left behind three squalling babies. There was a place in Canada where the Indians left five of them as a present. I was fretting.

God, You let me have good parents and I thank You. "Thank You for my brothers and sisters; they could have been worse. I even thank You for the latest squalling baby. Thank You, even if the Indians left us five of them." That's the prayer I said to You at school.

Lots of children walk around on Earth that don't know how they got there. Luckily, You gave us a good grandmother. She explained the mystery of babies to me. That was when our brother arrived. She took me to her house. I was crying because I wanted to go home and sleep in my own bed. Our grandmother took me on her old lap and she hugged me and said:

"I'm going to tell you the biggest secret. It's the secret of how babies are born. Tomorrow, when you wake up and go back to your house, you'll find a baby."

"Where does the baby come from?"

"I'm going to tell you the secret that came from my own grandmother. It's the secret that all the grandmothers in the country pass on to their grand-children. Later on you'll be a grandfather and your wife will be a grandmother, and she'll tell your grandchildren the secret."

"Where do babies come from?"

So then she started to whisper in my ear:

"You see, for a long, long time the Indians have known how to make beautiful wicker baskets. They come with their beautiful baskets that are woven like lace. Inside the basket they bring a baby. Only, before they go away again, they beat the *maman*. I had seventeen babies, who are all your uncles. I was beaten by the Indians seventeen times. That's why whenever a baby comes the *maman* has to stay in bed."

"Why do the Indians beat the *maman?*"

"I don't know; only papas know the answer."

After that I fell asleep, and I woke up later in the night because I was wetting my bed. God, will You explain how come I wet my bed every time there's a threat of a baby arriving?

Today at school, God, I was standing up in front of all the pupils in the class who knew that the Indians had come to beat our mother. I started to read. I knew our reading by heart. I didn't have to look at the letters. As I was saying the words, I thought about the new baby. I thought about how the Indians might have messed up my things when I was out of the house. I thought about our mother who might have her arms and legs broken in five or six places. I thought that I didn't really understand what was going on at our house with the baby and the Indians and our father who'd gone away to

Saint-Magloire-de-Bellechasse. All of a sudden I forgot to read and I realized I was peeing on the waxed school floor. Couldn't You send a miracle to cure me of peeing, God? When I fret too much I piss like a drainpipe. I'm not asking You to make me stop fretting, but please don't let me pee my pants so much.

After school, I came home all wet. In the baby's crib there was a new squaller. They told me it was a sister because it was dressed in pink. I didn't want to look. What do You expect me to say to a baby? And a sister's even worse. My mother was all pale in the bed. She told me she couldn't walk. I asked if the Indians had broken her legs. She said no. Her arms? She said no. Had the Indians wrung her neck like they did Big Red's mother? She said no. I thought the Indians had let her off pretty easy this time, even if she had to spend a whole week in bed.

They weren't as nice and gentle as I'd thought. Behind the house on the clothesline I saw sheets drying in the wind. They were still all red with blood. I think they beat our mother a little too hard.

Our father comes home on Saturday. I'll be going back to the house because our mother will need me. I want to be there. This has been a special day. I'll remember it for a long time.

God, I came to ask You not to send the Indians back to visit our mother too soon. I notice they're attracted mostly when our mother's fat. God, don't let her eat too much fudge. She won't get fat and the Indians won't be attracted and they won't come and beat her. And we won't have another squalling baby.

Roch
Carrier

4

Prayer about Forgetting

Today, God, I brought some red currants. Our grandmother wants to make wine, so I went out and picked currants and I tore my pants. The bushes were tough today. I tore my shirt, too. Our mother won't like that. She'll have to get out her spool of thread and do more mending. Sometimes it seems there isn't a day goes by that I don't rip the seat of my pants. God, why did You put thorns on shrubs and bushes? They make children get scratches on their legs and arms and rips in their clothes.

But thank You for Your currants. You made them round and firm and red this year. When our grandmother sniffs her glass of New Year's wine she'll burst out laughing and she'll say: "I feel as drunk as our grandfather Noah." Then she'll laugh even harder and say: "I think I've drunk too much wine. The red currants are crazy this year, crazy." Everybody will laugh until they choke. And then our grandmother will go and pour her wine down the sink: "I've had too much wine; I wouldn't want my grandchildren to see me the way our grandfather Noah dared to show himself!"

Now, the first time, I didn't know who this grandfather Noah was. He wasn't our grandfather. Noah wasn't anybody I'd ever seen in the village. I know now that he's the one who built the Ark during the Flood. He had a shipwreck on Mount Ararat; I saw it in the encyclopedia. . . . The first time I saw our grandmother throw away her nice red wine I said:

"*Mémère*, you didn't drink the wine, you only smelled it."

"Some things you shouldn't even smell!" she told me.

After our dinner, there were glasses with one drop or two drops of red currant wine all over the house. Sometimes there was a finger of wine in the bottom. Other times the glass was half full. I smelled them the way our grandmother did. It was a nice, perfumy smell: not like currants, but like some other fruit I didn't know. It smelled so good, I could have smelled that perfume all day long. It had a good smell like a tree all covered with beautiful fruit. It was the best thing I'd ever smelled. I wanted to drink it. So I drank every glass I found. The ones with a drop or two drops and the ones that were half full. There were a lot of glasses. Lots of people were there because it was New Year's Day.

I didn't turn soft and silly like our grandmother. I didn't turn funny, I didn't dance, I didn't sing or laugh, because I was too sleepy. The uncles, aunts and cousins had piled their coats in a bedroom. There were a lot of people so it made a mountain of wool and beaver fur and lynx and raccoon, a great mountain of silky hair, like Roger Lemelin says at the beginning of his book which is too long for me. I fell asleep like a bear in his bearskin.

This year, with those fine red currants You gave us, the wine will be even better. On New Year's Day our grandmother won't have to sniff for very long before she feels like laughing.

Our grandmother's birthday falls on New Year's Day. Every time the year gets young our grandmother gets older. I'm sure she thanks You for the red currants, too.

God, when You make currants like those, do You taste them to know how long to let them ripen, how much sun to give them, how much rain to make them drink? I can't imagine You just let them ripen on their own. When our mother or our grandmother cooks, she's always tasting with her finger until it tastes the way she likes it.

That's not why I came to see You today, to ask You that. I don't actually remember why I came in to pray. Anyway, thank You for the currants. I've never seen so many in my whole life. I really wish I could remember why I came here. Apparently, people start forgetting when they're old. Can a person be young and old at the same time?

Do You remember, God, when old Amadeus Tanguay forgot the name of his own wife? In the general store, all the old people were talking about the good old days when they were young. And old Amadeus wanted to talk about his wedding, when he was young; he'd married a young girl the same age as he was, who was also young. But when he tried to say the name of his wife, he'd forgotten it. Amadeus Tanguay had lived with his wife for a long time, his whole life, because he wasn't dead yet and neither was his wife. Practically a hundred years of life. After all that time, old Amadeus couldn't remember the name of his wife. He couldn't say it. His old friends were choking with laughter because they'd never heard of such a funny forgetting in their life. They all looked as if they'd had a lot of experience at forgetting. All of them weren't as young as Amadeus Tanguay, I mean they were older. Amadeus laughed along with his ancient friends because he thought the name of his wife would come back to his lips. It didn't come that morning.

Amadeus Tanguay went home and he still didn't know the name of his wife. He ate his soup with her and he wondered what her name was. At night he went to bed with her without knowing her name. He didn't dare to ask: "Wife, what's your name?" He was afraid he'd look like an old fool. He didn't sleep all night because of all the rummaging in his memory. It mustn't be very nice to sleep with your wife and not know her name.

The next day when he got up he still hadn't found it. He looked for it. He didn't talk. He didn't want to eat his morning porridge.

He set out for the general store. His friends gathered there every morning, always at the same time. He couldn't listen to their stories. All he could think about was the name of his wife. He didn't dare to talk. He was afraid of forgetting that he mustn't ask them for the name of his wife. He tried to find it. His face looked like a lot of worries.

Old Amadeus must have prayed to ask You to whisper the name of his wife in his ear. Or maybe he didn't pray, so You wouldn't think he'd turned into an old fool with a memory full of holes.

Apparently old Amadeus remembered the names of all the children in his grade one class, but not the name of his wife. Apparently he only went to grade one.

He spent all day walking from one end of the village to the other, his head down and not looking at anybody, he was so ashamed at what he'd forgotten. He wouldn't eat. He wasn't hungry. He didn't want to be sitting across from his wife who didn't have a name.

That night he went to bed again. He couldn't fall asleep beside his wife without a name. He just hoped he'd fall asleep from exhaustion.

All at once, he knew where he could find the name of his wife. He was relieved and reassured, as if he'd already found it. He congratulated himself for not going through the humiliation of asking his daughters or his daughters-in-law or their husbands for his wife's name. For the rest of his days he'd have had to listen to the story of "that time *Pépère* forgot *Mémère's* name" . . . Amadeus sat up in bed and announced:

"I'm sick. I have to go see the curé."

"Is it serious?" asked his wife.

"It's serious," was his reply.

"When it's serious, the curé's supposed to come and see the patient."

"It's too serious; this time the patient's going to the curé."

Up and dressed as if it was Sunday, though his worried wife kept trying to hold him back, old Amadeus went out. It was the darkest, blackest night.

He knocked at the door of Your priest. It took quite a while: it was night and the priest was asleep. We don't know if he was sleeping with his housekeeper. Nobody ever saw them sleeping together but lots of people wonder. They say that when there's a man and a woman it's in their nature to sleep together. I want to pray to You about that God, but later, if I don't forget.

Finally, the old priest came to the door, his mattress printed on his face. Old Amadeus said:

"Sorry to be coming by so early, but I'm an old man and I think I could die this very night, I'm that old. Before I do, I'd like to touch the page with my wedding on it in your big register, just touch the page and read it."

"Your health isn't good?" the priest asked, very concerned.

"No, I'm very sick. And in case I die I want to see the page in the register for the marriage I contracted sixty-three years ago . . . "

Your priest gave Amadeus a strange look. Then the old man almost lost his temper.

"If I can't see it before I die, I'll undo my marriage."

Your priest didn't understand, but since he wanted to get back into his bed as soon as possible, he said:

"Even at this impossible time of night, I can't refuse a good Roman Catholic French Canadian like you."

And he brought him the old marriage register. He found the page for the marriage of old Amadeus, who had a little trouble reading the name of his wife. But he managed, even though he'd forgotten his glasses.

"Euphémie! Euphémie! Good Lord, it's Euphémie!"

"I'll pray for you!" said the priest, closing the register and shoving old Amadeus toward the door.

He walked back down the hill and home. What joy there must have been in his heart! Anyone who saw him go past would have thought he was dancing, but everyone was asleep. I didn't see him myself, I'm just saying what the others said, how they thought it had happened. He came back to his house.

His wife was waiting for him at the door, worried.

"Feeling better now, Amadeus?"

He tried to reply:

"Euphémie, I'm all better!"

He was so full of happiness at having found the name of his wife, but when he tried to pronounce the name it wouldn't come to his lips. The name had dropped down in his memory again, like a small boat in a heavy sea. So then he said:

"I'm sick, I'm so sick! I'm too weak to even say your name . . . "

His wife was distraught. All her life she had loved this man. She probably loved him even more in his moment of weakness, our grandmother said. She took his arm and helped him walk to their bed.

"Don't tire yourself, don't say Euphémie, just call me Phémie."

"No, I'll call you Euphémie. I'm always going to call you Euphémie, I'll never forget it. Euphémie! My Euphémie! I'll never forget it."

"Don't say that. You're old, you know. So am I. And growing old is learning how to forget. A while ago, I spent a day and a night wondering what your name was, Amadeus. I'd forgotten it, as if I'd never seen you. And I didn't dare ask anybody. They'd have said: 'What an old fool! Forgetting her own husband's name!' And I didn't dare ask you, either. What would you have thought? For a day and a night, I was living in hell."

"Oh! I feel better," said old Amadeus. "And how did you remember my name?"

"I didn't want to ask our children or the sons-in-law or the daughters-in-law. So I went to the curé and looked in the marriage register."

"Yippee!" exclaimed old Amadeus, "I'm cured."

And he began to dance a jig as he had in the wild days of his youth.

"I'm cured, Phémie. Get out the red currant wine!"

God, I don't know why I'm telling You this story. I forgot. And I forgot that it's supper time. The soup must be on the table. I'm late.

Please, God, don't let there be too much forgetting in my life.

5

Titties
Prayer

God, I don't know if You, after You've eaten a meal, You lean back in your rocking chair and hibernate like our grandfather does. I wouldn't want to bother You about a pair of titties — but I saw two of them: a pair of two; two titties, I saw them, the whole thing, all round. I'm sorry if I woke You up from Your nap, God. It's on account of those two titties. I came here to confess that I saw two real live titties.

Before, I didn't know what titties were. Today I understood why they never say the word on the radio. If you say it you want to see. It would be so nice if You invented a kind of radio where people could see and hear at the same time. Then we could look at titties.

Your priest never says that word — at least not in church he doesn't. He's a holy man but I bet he's seen titties, too. If I've seen two, Your priest could have seen just as many, or even more. Maybe two dozen. Or less. I'm seven years old and I've seen two titties. Your priest must be sixty-one or sixty-two or sixty-three. Seven into sixty-three gives what? Nine. Nine times seven years old. I'm seven and I've seen two titties. Nine times seven equals sixty-three. Nine times two titties equals eighteen titties equals nine pairs. Your priest must have seen nine pairs of titties. I could never see that many in my whole life. And maybe he's seen more, or less, because the priest sees Heaven when he gazes at the Earth.

Seeing titties is so impressive, it must be a sin. God, I confess that I saw titties, but to tell You the truth, as soon as I've finished my prayer, which will be short, I'm going to run back and sit in the same place, outside the general store, in case there's more titties on display. I'll come back afterwards and pray to You. Please God, let me see two more titties. Seven years times four titties times nine.

When I'm sixty-three I'll have seen thirty-six titties. Eighteen pairs. Thank You God for inventing arithmetic.

Our mother has titties that I've never seen. Our father often goes out to the country to sell and buy. I don't know if he's even noticed that our mother has titties. Babies know. They're always squalling. When our mother can't stand it any more, she sighs and then she unbuttons her dress. After that she picks up the squaller, and what happens is like magic: the squaller disappears under a blanket. What do titties do to a baby? I guess that's a deep, dark secret.

I used to be a squalling baby too. And I used to cry and disappear under a blanket, but I don't remember a thing. God, why did You invent forgetting? I can remember the name of the capital of the Belgian Congo, but I can't remember our mother's titties.

Titties is a dirty word. When I hear it my cheeks go all red. I feel hot inside my ears and sometimes even at the bottom of my belly. Women never say that word. It's a man's word. You need dry ears to say it. Some children say it, too. Not girls though.

When girls hear it they shrug their shoulders and then they run away.

I say the word titties because I saw two of them. Seeing them, God, must be the same as not being wet behind the ears. Men always laugh after they say the word titties, as if it was the funniest thing in Your Creation.

At school, I took a really good look at the nun because, You see, the girls in my class are as flat as ironing boards. The nun wears so many dresses and slips and skirts and rosaries and veils you can't even tell if she's got titties underneath her bib. From what I hear, Your priest hasn't got a ding-dong under his soutane; maybe the nun hasn't got titties.

Learning about life isn't easy. I've been wondering for a long time how You made women's titties. Just wondering made me feel tickly, even in my ding-dong. When You were a little boy like me, God, You must have felt it too, didn't You?

I don't know why they make me learn the list of nouns that take "x" in the plural when I don't even know what a pair of titties is. You created the world in a really complicated way, God.

I'm going to tell You a story about titties. There was an unhappy widow that decided to die after her husband died. She took her dead husband's hunting rifle and she stuck the barrel two inches under her left titty because that's the side where the heart is. Then the unhappy woman pulled the trigger. A shot was fired. She didn't die. Two inches under her left titty, the bullet hit her knee.

Everybody in the general store laughed when they heard that story. So did I, even though I didn't understand it. I laughed as hard as a man. I was the last one to stop laughing. I told myself that one day I was going to see some real titties. I figured that titties aren't ordinary things like noses or ears or shoulder-blades.

The Laframboise boy, the one with a finger cut off, said there's some titties that jump in the air. He knows a woman that got two black eyes from running too fast. Her titties punched her in the eyes like fists. He says you have to harness titties because if they aren't tied down really tight they jump around like colts leaving the stable in the spring. I've seen young colts snorting and frisking in the spring. I tried to understand how women could have two spring colts inside their dresses.

You don't seem to mind, God, that Your Creation is hard to understand. Why do You want titties to be a mystery? When I was a squalling baby I drank from the mystery. Why have You erased my memories like mistakes in my dictation book?

Today, You showed me a pair of titties. Right after the apparition I was all red from head to toe, as if I'd been dipped in red paint. Real titties! Two. I saw them both, one beside the other! They weren't hard, they didn't look as if they had bones. They were as soft as cream. I couldn't look at them for very long. They were hanging inside the neckline of the dress. The strong midday sun, full of fire, was drenching them in light. They weren't round like balls, they were long, but not like cucumbers. They were more like eggs, big eggs sliced in two. They didn't look as if they had a shell. They moved like Jello. And there's something at the end like chocolates. Now that I've seen them, God, I know what a sin is. My head was as dizzy as if I'd spun around a hundred times. Or more. I couldn't run because

I couldn't walk: my legs felt as if they'd been cut off.

She saw me look. I could tell that she knew I was red. She didn't do up her blouse. I felt as if there were feathers tickling me all over my whole body from head to toe, and even inside my body, but it was mostly in my pants that the feathers were tickling, in a place I mustn't say because we're in Your church. But it's You that created that place so I'm going to tell You where it tickled: my ding-dong. I didn't like it. I can't wait to grow up. I won't feel that tickling any more.

I don't need to tell You how it happened, God, because it was You that made it happen. It was You that offered me titties in Your invisible hand.

Children who don't observe get bored. I spend whole days looking. I don't get bored because I learn. You can't get bored when you're learning. If I keep looking, I think I'll finally see You, God, even if You're invisible.

Every year there's a kind of Gypsies that come to the village. They come to sell little wicker tables or chairs. They come to tell the future or to sell magic medicines to cure diseases that Dr Robitaille can't do anything for. They don't seem to know anything about new cars. They always drive rusty, battered old jalopies with writing scrawled over them that's full of mistakes, like real ignoramuses. They know lots of secrets ordinary people wish they knew. Gypsies can pile at least twice as many people in their cars as ordinary people can. After our father piles the children and our mother and our father in his Ford, we can't fit any more in. The Gypsies though, they can fit as many people in a car as in a bus.

Today it was a rusty panel truck that pulled up outside the general store. I was lying on my stomach in the grass. I was spying on life. There was rust all over, even on the brakes of the truck, and they screeched like a girl having a tooth pulled. And then the father Gypsy, with his long black hair and his pointed boots and a belt around his shirt instead of his pants, came to open the back door of his panel truck. The door didn't just open, it fell on the ground. The father Gypsy started kicking the door with his pointed boots. He was probably swearing but not in our language; it was in his language.

God, do You understand cursing and swearing when they're in a foreign language?

A fat woman got down from the cab, carrying a suitcase, and barefoot, with dirty feet that haven't seen soap since last year, and a long skirt with bright colours and ruffles and pleats and ribbons. And a great big suitcase, like I already told You. Then I saw children get out, as many as if they were getting off a train: all sizes, all sexes, black hair, bare, dirty feet. All the girls had long skirts with ruffles, very long black hair and lots of necklaces that clinked, and squalling babies in their arms.

The last one arrived. She was tall. She had to bend over to get out. Then I saw, God! It was like lightning in your face. I saw those titties I told You about.

God, forgive my sin. Just confessing it is making me tickle again where I can't say. Forgive my tickle sin. Forgive my titties sin. Please God, let me see some others.

Thank You, God, for making titties appear to me. Now I understand one mystery in Your Creation.

6

Writing
Prayer

Today, God, I confess that I have sinned with chalk. The nun at school gave me a reprimand, the worst one since the village was founded in 1862. I came in to see You before I go home. Our mother will likely try to outdo the nun.

Our father comes home tonight. It's been two weeks since he went away. Please God give me the courage to go home.

I didn't do anything, God. All I did was write. Is writing a sin? Writing is the best thing to do in the world, after looking out the window. When I write, I always look out the window. When people pray they look out the window, too. Praying and writing are a little bit the same. When you write, you look up at the sky every two or three words.

That's where I find my most beautiful words when I write my compositions.

I like to write. When you write you invent the things you want, with the people you want and colours you choose for yourself. Like You when You created the world. Writing is my version of the Creation of the world.

The other day I wrote in my composition: "Now I will take you to visit my golden castle, which is held up on the strong shoulders of the very powerful black, hunchbacked dwarfs who stand at the four corners." Just like that. God, You know that I don't have a castle, I don't have gold and I don't have four dwarfs. But it wasn't a lie. Because I was writing! If I'd said all that when I was talking it would have been a lie. Writing isn't lying. My castle in the composition is a creation, like Yours, God; the only difference is that Yours exists.

And I didn't lie today, either. The nun at school asked:

"What happened to the chalk?"

Everybody mumbled "I don't know." I knew where the chalk was but I didn't mumble. I didn't say anything. When you don't say anything, it's not lying. Lying means telling a falsehood. And if you don't tell a falsehood, it means you're telling the truth.

The real truth is that I took the box of chalk: it's a beautiful wooden box with a sliding lid and sticks of chalk stacked like cordwood. Our nun thought that another nun had come and borrowed her chalk. She wasn't happy about it, but she didn't say anything more about the chalk. It was beautiful white chalk. The box was full. I'd hidden it in my bag.

That may sound like theft, God, but chalk is made for writing. What I did was to write with the chalk.

Drawing is hard. You have to flatten life out and then stick it on the paper. I learned how to write faster than I learned anything else: using a knife and fork, putting my hand over my mouth when I cough, standing on my feet to walk and skate, peeing somewhere else besides my bed. It took me months of efforts to learn those things. I learned how to write in a few weeks.

The nun at school told us it was You who whispered the idea of writing to the holy prophets. If You invented the idea of writing the Bible after You created the world, it means You thought there was something missing in the world that You'd created. Thank You, God, for inventing books.

Lots of children in the world, and even here in the village, don't know how to read and write. Thank You, God, for giving me reading and writing.

God, it's true that I borrowed the chalk . . . When you borrow something you're supposed to put it back, but chalk wears out. On cement, it wears out and disappears like dust. Forgive me God, because I can't give the chalk back to the nun.

The other day I danced along the sidewalk on my way to school. I was so happy. I skipped and skipped, I was as silly as a little dog that plays because it's glad to be alive. All of a sudden I got an idea. I thought the sidewalk was a wonderful invention for walking, but that it could be used for something else. I stopped dancing and skipping so

I could think a little harder. A few minutes later, I decided that I'd need a lot of chalk.

After school I ran down the sidewalk from one end of the village to the other. I went to the other side of the hill, as far as the house of the lady that sells cloth for sewing, and from there I went to the house of the man that goes to the farms to taste what the cows' cream tastes like. I went past Your chapel, past the bank, past Your church, past the butcher shop, past the post office, past Dr Robitaille's house, past the pool hall, past the sleigh factory and past the other chapel, and I counted all the squares. You know how the sidewalk's divided into squares? If it had been poured in just one strip, the sidewalk would be shattered by the frost. That's why the men built it in square sections.

I'm going to ask You a riddle, God: how many squares are there in the village sidewalk? I'll give You the answer. The sidewalk is divided into six hundred and sixty-eight squares. When I was walking, I got the idea that I could write one letter in every square: six hundred and sixty-eight letters. I'd need a whole box of chalk, at least.

The nun didn't give us any homework because it's the birthday of the little saint who flogged himself with his belt when he got undressed. He's a model for young people, the nun told us. Somebody who whips himself with his belt is no example, unless you're looking for an example of a raving lunatic. God, did You create us and put us on Earth so we could flog ourselves with our belts? It's not worth becoming a saint if you become a raving lunatic. A model for young people, God, is an inventor. You invented the world. I'd like to imitate You. You were right to invent life, instead of flagellating Yourself with a belt.

I was thinking about all that as I was walking. I was thinking that You had the vault of Heaven, while I had the sidewalk. You wrote Your message in the sky. On a clear night, the stars look like writing. I don't know how to read them yet, but when I'm bigger I'm going to learn other languages and maybe the language of Your Bible also, because that's the language You must have used when You wrote Your messages in the sky.

I didn't have any stars, but I could get some

chalk. That's why I decided to write on the sidewalk. The street would have been dangerous. There aren't as many cars here as there are in town, but there's also not as big a choice of children to run down.

But what should I write? I'd have liked to give the people in the village some reflection to read, something to make them think, like the priest does at Mass, or the editor of the newspaper *Action catholique*.

When I'm grown up I'm going to write important messages too.

I'm a child, and I can't know as much as Your Bible or the person who invented atoms or the cement that's as hard as the rocks You made. So I decided that the message I would write on the sidewalk would be: "WHAT TIME IS IT?" I was proud of myself. Everybody would be interested in that question. Everybody would try to answer it. I'd see everybody rummage in their pockets or raise their wrists to look at their watches. It would be really funny.

I was glad, but not for long. I decided I was pretty

brainless. Is it worth the trouble of being born and learning how to walk and write when the only question you can come up with is "What time is it?" I was ashamed. It was time to go home for supper.

After supper I went back and walked down the sidewalk, from end to end, and once again I counted all the squares. On my way there I counted 628. The first time I'd counted 668. There was a mistake; I decided to check. On my way back from the other end of the sidewalk, I counted 722 squares. The sidewalk is made of cement. It isn't something you can pull out like an accordion. I wasn't very proud of myself: I couldn't count and I couldn't write.

I was too ashamed. God, I want to become an inventor of something and have my picture in the encyclopedia, or someone who does good works and hurts bad people, but I can't even count. In our room, I didn't think I'd be able to get to sleep. I was discouraged. I started biting my pillow. I felt like crying but I didn't want to cry. Finally I cried. My pillow was as wet as a dishcloth. I slept like a log, just as if I still had all my pride.

When I woke up there was a dream still clinging to the inside of my head like a spider-web on a corner of the fence. (The nun at school gives me good marks when I write comparisons like that.) I woke up with the idea that when I'm grown up, I'll invent wonderful stories like Hans Christian Andersen in the encyclopedia. That idea made me as happy as a little bird. I decided to start right away to be a great writer like Hans Christian Andersen, even though I haven't got a big nose like his.

I pretended to get washed, I pretended to eat my cereal, and then I took my box of chalk and ran to the end of the sidewalk, past the house of the man who tastes the cows' cream. I was on my way to becoming a great writer. I drew my first block letters. I was so happy, God; I think I could go on writing for the rest of my life. It was a lot more fun than winning a hockey game or catching a trout or snaring a hare. It was my hand that was writing but I felt dizzy all over my whole body, like the time I danced at our uncle's wedding. On each of the squares in the sidewalk I wrote one letter. It was a letter from the name of one of the pupils in my class. I like the pupils in my class. Writing their names was writing the finest thing I could invent. That was the idea I woke up with.

Then I wrote as fast as I could: Émery Lessard, Roger Tanguay, Valmont Mathieu, Lucien Ménard, Claude Bédard, Adéodat Dorval, Martine Labbé, Bibiane Vachon, Bibiane Cloutier, René Bédard, Ernest Bissonnette, Rita Lachance, Rénelle Lacroix. I cheated, God, because I also wrote the names of our brothers and our sisters, but I forgot my own.

All at once somebody asked me:

"What are you doing?"

"Writing," I said.

It was Your priest, God. So then I decided to write Your name.

"So you're writing, are you?" Your priest repeated.

Your priest didn't look very proud of me. So then I wrote his name. He didn't seem any happier. He asked:

"Haven't you got a scribbler to write in?"

"It's fun to write on the sidewalk."

"My child, many people who had fun writing have found themselves in Hell."

When I got to school the nun was waiting for me with weapons.

"Monsieur le curé phoned to say you'd scribbled all over the sidewalk."

"No, I only wrote on 338 squares."

"The sidewalk is a public thoroughfare, and you've dirtied the public thoroughfare."

"Writing isn't dirty."

"My child, you have a lot to learn . . ."

She gave me a bucket of water. It was much too heavy. I spilled a little water. She also gave me a mop. And I went to erase everything I'd written. The whole village watched me mop up my writing. I've never been so humiliated in my life. If Hans Christian Andersen had had to erase his writing we'd never have known his stories. I'd never have seen his big nose in the encyclopedia.

I'm going to stop praying to You now, God. I've told You how I washed away my chalk sin.

7

Prayer for
a Wad of
Dollar Bills

Today, God, I wished I had a wad of dollar bills in the back pocket of my short pants. Please God, let me be very rich! Or even a little rich. I promise I'll help our grandfather.

I was with our grandfather in his blacksmith shop today. He put me in charge of the bellows. I'd climbed up on an old chair. He was holding a big iron ring in the fire, to make a wagon wheel. I was pumping air with the bellows. It was practically a hurricane. You've seen one, God: the bellows looks like a big accordion made out of cow's hide leather. It doesn't play music; it blows. The fire was dancing around. Our grandfather said: "Harder! Harder!" I pumped faster and faster. There were hardly any flames, just red coals like where the Devil lives. The iron was so red it was almost white. Our grandfather told me: "I couldn't've done such a good job without a little man to help me."

Our grandmother arrived. She only comes to the shop on important occasions. When he saw her, our grandfather told me: "Now give me the bellows: at this stage the fire needs an experienced man."

I'd rather have been in charge of blowing on the fire so our grandmother could see me working, but I'm little and when people tell me "Go away!" I have to do as I'm told.

Our grandmother said: "Our boy's going off to college, and we can't send him without a stitch. We can't send him in his country clothes, because he's going to be studying with the sons of notaries and doctors. We have to have a suit made for him."

Our grandfather said: "You're right, wife, we'll have to have a suit made for our boy." He stopped working the bellows and started to look for his hammer. He couldn't see it, even though it was on the anvil right in front of his eyes. I said: "The hammer's right in front of your eyes on the anvil." He looked at the anvil and he couldn't see the hammer. So then I picked up the hammer in both hands and gave it to him. He took it and then put it back on the anvil. The iron in the forge had turned black again. Our grandfather's mind was elsewhere.

Our grandmother said: "I saw the seamstress. She took our boy's measurements. I'll provide the black serge, and the seamstress will charge us ten dollars. That makes a total of twenty dollars to dress our boy."

"Twenty dollars . . . " our grandfather repeated.

"Twenty dollars," our grandmother confirmed.

"Be cheaper if he went around bare-bummed like they do in Africa where the missionaries are. . . . But when you're baptized you hide your bum. Especially in winter," our grandfather joked.

Then he repeated: "Twenty bucks."

He started looking for his tobacco and he couldn't find it. After he found it, he couldn't find his pipe. And when he found his pipe in his pocket, he couldn't remember where he'd lost his tobacco. And the iron was getting cold. He'd have to start the job over. I thought: our grandfather's worried about something.

"Yup," he said, "our boy needs a suit. Only thing is, I bought wood for the shop, coal for the forge and iron for the wheelwright's shop. The supplier won't let a nail or a match leave his warehouse unless I pay cash on the barrel. Everything I earned this summer I spent on materials for the fall. Twenty dollars is a fortune. I remember when the seamstress made a suit for five."

"She asks twenty now, but it's good for several years. When the suit's too small for our boy, the other one can jump into it."

"I ain't got twenty bucks," our grandfather decided. "So our boy won't be getting any suit made."

All of a sudden, he found his tobacco and his pipe and he went back to work at the bellows. The fire exploded under the coal and the coal turned red again.

Our grandfather told me: "Climb back up on that old chair and pump like a man!"

I grasped the handle and I started pumping the air as if I was responsible for a wind storm.

Our grandmother was there. I wanted her to see me so she could be proud of me. God, she didn't even notice me. She repeated: "Our boy needs to have a suit made and it costs twenty dollars."

I probably wasn't pumping fast enough for my grandfather's liking. He grabbed the handle of the bellows and he pumped so hard that I was going up and down along with it. I didn't let go. I was afraid I'd fall off the old chair and break my backside.

Our grandmother said: "It's been seven or eight years Lassouche has owed you twenty dollars. This'd be the time to get paid back."

"I've got my pride. I'm not asking Lassouche for charity like a beggar."

"You don't give a beggar twenty dollars," I told them, "you give a penny."

"Pump!" said our grandfather.

God, he never used to yell at me like that. I felt as if he hated me. But I don't think he hated me.

"Our boy can't go around in rags and feel humiliated," said our grandmother. "He needs a suit. It costs twenty dollars. Lassouche owes you twenty dollars."

"It's been seven, eight, ten years. He's forgotten. He'll think I want to rob him."

"And he's not robbing you by pretending to forget? He's like us, he's thought about our twenty dollars every night before he goes to sleep."

"Lassouche is honest," our grandfather cut in. "If he owed me twenty dollars, he'd have paid off his debt by now. I think we're making a mistake. Lassouche doesn't owe us any twenty dollars."

Our grandfather was practically furious. There was so much air in the bellows, the coal was rolling in the forge. When the Devil gets mad, God, Hell must be really red!

"I'm taking the serge to the seamstress," said our grandmother. "And you, you go and collect that twenty dollars from Lassouche."

Our grandfather let out a sigh that was practically as loud as the bellows, and then he ran his big hand over my hair. It was strong, but soft. Our grandfather said: "Get down off your chair, we're going to the Lassouche house, you and me."

"Does Lassouche," I asked him, "does he owe you twenty dollars?"

"He's owed me twenty dollars since the twenty-third of May in the year you were born. Lassouche is going to pay me back today or I'll choke him with my right hand."

Our grandfather's always said that his right hand is stronger than his left. God, I was proud of our grandfather who wanted to choke Lassouche to get back his twenty dollars to have our uncle's suit made!

We walked to the Lassouche house without talking. I didn't want to disturb his thinking. He looked pretty mean. All of a sudden he said: "Little fellow, you think you could help me? . . . You think you could say: 'Monsieur Lassouche, you owe us twenty dollars. We've come to get paid. We won't charge any interest'?"

If I'd been a girl I'd have jumped in our grandfather's arms to give him a hug. I was glad to help him!

Yes, I'll remember all my life: "Monsieur Lassouche, you owe us twenty dollars. We've come to get paid. We charge interest of three and one-eighth percent per year."

There's a lot of Lassouche children but not many hens or cows. You can't tell what they live on. Apparently they put water in their milk. The Lassouche father always wears a white shirt that's starched like a nun's bib. Nobody in the village can remember ever seeing him with his hands dirty from work. He's never had a drop of sweat on his brow. He's a man who thinks and raises a big flock of children and knows important people in the government in Quebec City. Premier Duplessis even gave him a cigar. The Lassouche father had it framed. Today, the Lassouche father took us and showed us Duplessis's cigar, framed on the living-room wall above the crucifix. It's a big cigar.

The Lassouche father often goes to the big city of Quebec, but the Lassouche mother stays in the village like all our mothers. She's proud of her husband. She washes at least three white shirts a day. We see them drying outside in the wind. She always walks six or seven paces behind him. She doesn't like getting dressed up; she dresses as if she was poor. The Lassouche father dresses better than Premier Duplessis. With his high-placed friends, he knows all the secrets they don't tell on the radio or in the papers. He learned about the declaration of war two or three weeks before everybody else.

Anyway, he's bald except for some hairs on the top of his head. He combs them with hair grease to paste them against the skin. He pretends that he's educated because he pretends he doesn't know how to curse You, God.

The paint's been off his shingle house ever since Christopher Columbus discovered America in 1492. If You make the wind blow too hard, God, the roof could sail away like a kite.

Our grandfather didn't dare to knock at the door because the whole thing could have collapsed like a house of cards. We went inside. The Lassouche father came and shook our hands as if we were company. Our grandfather said: "My little fellow's got something to say to you."

"Monsieur Lassouche," I said, "you owe us twenty dollars. We've come to get paid. We charge interest of thirty-eight percent a year."

Then I stepped back behind our grandfather and our grandfather said: "My little fellow's told you how things stand."

The Lassouche father, in his white shirt and tight necktie, pulled out two chairs for us and said: "These are ideal circumstances for talking about money. Take a minute and sit down. I've some good tobacco that was given to me personally by the Minister of Roads, who I saw recently. I looked him in the eye like I'm looking at you, and he gave me the tobacco that he'd received personally from the American president of the Canadian Digging Company. That company's going to dig a tunnel under the St Lawrence River. It's a big hole, two miles long and high enough for trucks and trains. One dollar invested in that hole is a dollar that'll multiply by a hundred, a thousand. Bridges are finished; they fall down, they're dangerous, because the Communists could blow them up. The Minister of Roads told me himself: tunnels are the way of the future."

The Lassouche father talked for a long time. Our grandfather listened for a long time. Me too, I listened; sometimes I pretended to understand.

Finally our grandfather decided we were going. On the doorstep the Lassouche father said: "I'd be cheating you if I gave you a measly twenty-dollar bill today, even with annual interest of thirty-eight percent. Instead, I'm going to have it invested for you personally by the American president of Canadian Digging. The interest will be one thousand percent guaranteed."

Then I saw our grandfather take out a twenty-dollar bill he had rolled up in his tobacco pouch. He handed it to the Lassouche father:

"I wouldn't want to appear too rich, but I'd like to put this twenty dollars in the hole too. With all that interest, I'll be able to buy my boys an education and get suits made for them."

"Twenty bucks in the tunnel under the St Lawrence River," declaimed the Lassouche father, "is an investment as safe as indulgences in the bank of Heaven."

God, I have a prayer for You: please don't let it turn out that our grandfather got screwed.

8

The
Hanged Man's
Prayer

Is it true, God, that when a hanged man is hanged he catches diarrhoea? The men in the village said that everything the hanged man ate in the past five days ended up in his pants. I'd just as soon not see that. Our father said:

"Hanging's a good remedy for constipation."

The hanged man, before he was a hanged man, had bad problems. You must know what they are. Everything that happens on Earth happens because You want it. Apparently, not one hair falls from my head without Your holy permission. Your priest said so in church.

As far as I'm concerned, I think that You are infinitely good, infinitely kind, and that You can only bring good to the Earth. All the evil must be sent by the Devil. But apparently that isn't true. If

You send evil to the Earth, can the Devil send good? Excuse me, God, I don't mean to spit insults at You, but I really wish somebody would tell me the plain truth. Why don't You write a book that explains how the world works, the way the *Encyclopédie de la jeunesse* explains steam engines?

The hanged man must have talked to You about his problems. He had more problems in one week than you see in the newspaper in a month. He must have prayed to You. Why did You bombard him with bad luck? Did You try to give him the strength of heart to bear his sorrow and hardships? If You saw the poor hanged man tie a knot around his neck, You should have said: "Go ahead, hanged man, but I'm going to send you another problem: your rope will break and you'll fall down and break your nose!"

When You saw the rope pulled tight and jerking because the hanged man was twitching around, why didn't Your hand give a little flick with a knife and break the rope? Even if the hanged man didn't pray to You, You should have helped him. You are good and perfect and You can understand people who aren't good and perfect. If You didn't help the hanged man, God, You'll have to explain why not.

I tell myself that if the hanged man had received Your help, he wouldn't be a hanged man. I don't understand. Life is too big for my little head.

Everybody's talking about the hanged man. So even if nobody wants to tell the children anything, we children just have to listen. That's how come I know everything. Thank you for giving me big ears.

The hanged man used to work in the forest all winter, far away, in Abitibi. He'd leave during deer-hunting season, and then he'd come back just before the snow melted. This year, he got an urge to come back that came over him all of a sudden like a stomachache, in the middle of February. Nobody could keep him up at the camp. He was drawn to his house the way a fish out of water is drawn to the river (if he lives in a river, or the sea if he lives in the sea). So the hanged man came home.

He went inside his house. His children were there, five or six of them, the little ones; the big ones were in the barn. The hanged man's wife was in the bedroom. That's where the hanged man found her, in the bed, with a man from another parish who makes illegal beer out of grapes and bugs. There was a battle, with broken windows and broken teeth and shouting. It wasn't very nice, God!

The hanged man came out of the bedroom and hit the little children, who hadn't done anything. They were squalling as if he'd put them through the meat-grinder.

The hanged man's wife and the man who makes beer were in bed in the middle of the day. The people in the village said they weren't sleeping. Maybe they were just tired. The man who makes beer must have his own bed at home, so why would he sleep in the hanged man's?

After that, the hanged man went out to the stable, crying and cursing. He hadn't visited his cows since before the snow fell in November and he wanted to see how the calves were doing. There was a smell of tobacco in the barn. It was his children, the bigger ones, who were smoking in the hay. The hanged man gave them a hiding because they were too young to smoke. Then he lit into them again because the hay was too dry and you aren't supposed to smoke in dry hay.

There were no animals. Where were the animals? Out in the snow? In the cold? No. The animals had been caught by a germ and they were all dead. The stable was empty. It was You, God, who created the germs that made them sick. . . . Why?

The hanged man couldn't tolerate so much bad luck. He wanted to forget his life: forget the cows and calves he'd lost; forget that his wife was sleeping in the middle of the day with the man who makes beer; forget that his children went outside and hid so they could smoke in the hay. The hanged man told You, God:

"I'm going to drink like You've never seen anybody drink."

The hanged man drank for two or three days; he was sick for two or three days. Then he realized that he was still alive. Not a soul in the village wanted to talk to him. As soon as he showed up anywhere, people fell silent. They turned their backs as if he was a nightmare in the flesh.

Everybody knew something the hanged man didn't know. A fire had started in the hay because of the children who'd gone back to smoke. The barn had burned down with the children smoking inside. The fire had leapt up onto the roof of the house and devoured everything: the sick children and the wife who was still in bed in the middle of the day with the man who makes illegal beer out of grapes and bugs.

God, You bring children into the world and then You toss them on the fire like logs. That's worse than throwing them into Hell. Why did You give them life and then turn around and take it away? If the hanged man's wife hadn't been in bed in the daytime, she could have at least stopped her youngest from burning, but she'd locked the door in case her husband showed up in the middle of everything. Everybody fried. When the hanged man came back, he didn't have to bang on the door to break it down. All that was left was a pile of black ashes in the snow. Outside, there was the sleigh that belonged to the man who made illegal beer. But not his horse. He'd unhitched it. The animal had burned in the stable. Afterwards, the men found his four shoes in the ashes. They also found the watch that belonged to the man who made illegal beer. It had baked in the ashes like a potato.

When the hanged man saw that he said:

"I've seen too many things in my life. I don't want to see anything else."

The stable hadn't all burned down: a few charred beams and a few posts were still standing, black and sad. The hanged man found a rope hanging from the beer man's sleigh. He wound one end of it around a beam. Then he wound the other end around his neck, and the hanged man hanged himself. When a man prefers death to life, it must be hard to persuade him that life is beautiful.

The men who found the hanged man swaying from his rope in the rubble of the stable couldn't understand how he'd managed to get himself up there. "When somebody's looking for death," they said, "he can always figure out a way to find it." The hanged man was swaying in the wind. He was frozen as hard as ice. His shit was frozen, so it didn't have any smell.

God, why do You send such sad things to Earth? Sad things belong in Hell, not on Earth. I'm sorry, God, I don't want to tell You what to send to the Earth, but it's where I live, so I'm just giving you my preferences. Anyway, if I was You, I . . . I wouldn't have inflicted (that's in the dictionary) the hanged man with so many problems. He was a good man before he got to be so unhappy. But I'm not You and I'm way too small to understand what goes on inside Your great eternal head.

The men took down the hanged man and they laid him in a sleigh and drove him to the priest to be buried. But the priest said:

"The hanged man didn't die like a Catholic, he died like a dog. I can't bury him in the cemetery along with Catholics who died a Catholic death. He has to be buried like a dog."

God, I've never heard of a dog that hanged itself. Only a human being can do that. But the priest said the hanged man had died like a dog. When Your priest talks, it's You who's talking. The nun told us that in school. God, I don't think a dog could hang itself out of sadness.

The priest didn't want to insult the Catholic dead by letting the hanged man who didn't die a Catholic death be buried with them. The men laid his corpse, that was as stiff as a log, in the sleigh and went from house to house to ask for hospitality. The hanged man was imported from two or three parishes away. He didn't have any family in the village. At every door they asked permission to bury him on their land. The hanged man had attracted so much trouble during his life on Earth that everybody thought he'd attract even more during his eternal life. He'd refused to suffer the way a Catholic is supposed to suffer. Is our religion the best, God, because it's the one where you suffer the most?

The hanged man hasn't been buried yet. Nobody wants to give him hospitality on their land. Luckily, the cold will keep him as hard as ice. If You give us mild weather, God, the hanged man will melt. Tonight they put him in the Laframboise hayloft. "Just one night," said old man Laframboise. "Just one night."

It's horrible to look at somebody you've seen alive and who's looking at you, frozen by cold and death. The worst disaster You send, God, is death.

Our little sister thinks that dead people aren't dead. She thinks that the dead go walking across the Earth like they did when they were alive. When she thinks about that, she gets so scared she turns white. She imagines seeing dead people in her bedroom, in her closet, under her bed, dead people who walk through the night like fish in the water. I think that when you're dead, you're dead. . . .

Maybe not completely dead. . . . Maybe the dead come back to Earth to finish off what they couldn't finish when they were alive. If You can give life to those who don't have it, You can certainly give back life to those who've lost it. Maybe whatever dies doesn't die completely. Sometimes I'm afraid of the dead too: they seem too quiet. . . .

But I'm not nearly as scared as our little sister. She saw the hanged man, too. I was sure she wouldn't sleep that night, that she'd hear him creaking across her bedroom floor, that she'd see his fingers and his big nails scratch at the window in her room.

I thought I could have some fun. Sometimes you feel like laughing. . . . I took a coat-hanger. I hung our father's work pants on it. I tied boots to the pants. I draped a shirt over the hanger. And I hung the hanger in the closet. When our little sister opened the door, she saw the hanged man. She yelled so loud, we laughed our heads off.

We didn't laugh very long. Our mother talked to us so loud that I decided to come and confess to You, because I'd committed the sin of the hanged man.

Our sister was howling tears as if she'd swallowed the whole Famine River. Our father took our little sister in his arms and held her really tight, as if he was our mother.

Death is scary for children, God. Why did You create it?

9

Camp-
stove
Prayer

Hello, God. I came to apologize about the camp-
stove. Our father wasn't very happy. He kept saying
over and over:

"What are we going to do with him?"

"Him" was me. Our father got very upset. He
was very mad. When our father gets mad his cheeks
turn red. He started running after me. He was
running because I was running away. And I was
running away because he wanted to spank my
backside. I could hear him breathing behind me.

I'd rather have my backside punished by a long,
long spanking than be tossed into the fires of Hell.
Hell isn't a very great invention, if you ask me. The
creator of apple trees and strawberries and birds and
fish shouldn't have created Hell. . . .

Our father was furious; I really think he would

have liked to create Hell just to throw me inside. Our father's always red when he gets mad. Suddenly I saw him turn white: as white as a ghost on the night of November first. His mouth was open as wide as if he'd shouted, but he didn't have any voice. At the same time, his two hands were clutching his belt as if his belly was too heavy to carry. He stopped. Now I didn't have to run away.

Our mother arrived and accused me:

"You're trying to kill your father!"

I didn't want to kill our father. I told my mother. Instead of being happy, she turned as pale and furious as my father. She wanted to collapse into the rocking chair, but our father was already there. So she said to me:

"And you want to kill your mother too. . . . "

I don't want to kill our mother, either. You know that, deep in my heart, I want our mother and our father to live for a long time. I want to have children, later on. My children will have children. Their children will have children. I'd like our mother and our father to live long enough to rock them all. They'll certainly die before that.

Death isn't Your best invention, either. Nobody's happy to die. Even people who are very old when they die don't like it. Even people who take their own lives with a rope around their necks; dying makes them as unhappy as living did. God, if You invented life I'm sure You could disinvent death. And then our parents would stop saying:

"Do you want to kill us?"

I'm sure they know that I don't want them to die. Why do they say I do? They must mean something else, and they don't know how to say it. Couldn't You help them a little to learn how to talk to me?

After they said: "Do you want to kill us?" I took a look at my face in the mirror when I was washing my hands. I thought I looked like the picture of the murderer in the newspaper. God, I don't want to kill them.

I promise You: the next time my father chases me when I've done something I shouldn't, I'm going to let him catch me and I'll let him dislocate my behind. I'd rather have a sore bum than see my father suffocate.

God who seest (that's in my grammar book) everything that happens on Earth, You know my father's camp-stove. He couldn't get through a winter without his camp-stove. I've never seen my father so happy as when his camp-stove fills the little shed on the back of his sleigh with its fragrant heat.

When he goes to the villages on the other side of the mountain, to Saint-Magloire-de-Bellechasse, everybody knows our father. And everybody knows his yellow sleigh-shed with his name painted on the sides in big red and black letters. He carts around in it everything he's going to sell on the farms: his flasks of medicines for the cows, his bags of candies for the calves, his boxes of vitamins for the pigs. Our father's proud of his sleigh-shed. His chair has sheepskin upholstery, but he doesn't sit in it. He stays standing up so he can see the people watching him go by. He greets everybody by taking off his otter-skin cap. His horse looks even prouder than he does. Our father dresses him up with a fine harness decorated with a whole hardware store-full of shiny ornaments and a whole jewellery shop of sleigh-bells. The horse seems to know he's got the nicest harness in the Appalachians. He does his work with a smile. His sleigh-shed is the only one of its kind in the whole region. He's a famous horse; that must make him happy. And behind him he can smell the piled-up bags of oats. His master's never given him the whip. Our father makes his whip whistle in the air so he'll look like a master, but You know, God, that the whip has never touched the horse's rump. The animal's happy: he's never been humiliated like other horses in the region.

Our father's famous because of the smoke that comes out of the sleigh-shed. It's a fine thing to see: a black horse, with bells, pulling through the sparkling white snow a yellow sleigh-shed with our father standing up and wearing his otter-skin cap. Overhead there's a little cloud of white smoke — that's the sign the sleigh-shed leaves in the sky. When I'm at school, I sometimes see our father go by in his sleigh-shed, and then I feel proud. It isn't a sin to feel proud of your father, is it God?

There wouldn't be any smoke if there wasn't a fire in the sleigh-shed. Our father doesn't like to

freeze his nose. Outside, snow and icicles hang
from the roofs, and trees crack in the cold. Inside
the sleigh-shed, it's warm. Our father likes the
warmth of a good wood fire. He had a stove made
and he feeds it maple wood. The stove turns red
with the heat; its belly is swollen with fire. There's
sweat underneath our father's cap. Outside, there's
ice; at the windows there's frost. Inside, it's like the
sun at the Equator. The camp-stove gets rid of its
smoke through the little chimney that sticks out of
the roof.

   I'm sure You don't need a camp-stove up in
Heaven. If You know what's in the hearts of men,
You must know that a camp-stove isn't like a
cooking stove in the kitchen. It's made out of an
empty barrel that sits on four iron feet. Our father's
camp-stove is little, but it gives off so much heat!
Sometimes our father invites me inside with him,
but I'd rather walk behind the sleigh-shed. It's not
that I don't love our father, God, but I hate being
hot. With his sheep-fur boots, his sheepskin vest,
his coonskin coat, his otter-skin cap, his wool-lined
leather mitts and the warmth of his camp-stove,

our father must feel like a tomcat purring in the July sun.

Not everybody's warm like that in winter. Some poor people haven't got a fur coat or a sheepskin vest. Some houses are very cold. The other day, I was listening to the men at the general store. They were talking about a house nearby where poor people live; it's so badly built that the snow comes in through the planks in the wall when there's a storm. There's ice on the walls inside. One day the children couldn't go to school because they couldn't get their clothes down off the nails in the wall; they were frozen in the ice. That house is crammed full of children. And grandparents, too, who are cold. It seems that being poor makes you live to a ripe old age. All those poor people are cold inside that cold house. The children are so cold their faces are blue. The old people will cough to death because they have colds that don't get better. There are twenty-seven in the Laframboise family. A man in the general store said that when the wind blows, the lamp in their house goes out. They're too poor to dress all the children, so some of them go around naked when the others are dressed. It's the same thing for food. One day one of them eats, and the next day he doesn't because it's someone else's turn.

The Laframboise children go to our school. I'm not happy that they're cold. I've never been cold. Our house is always as warm as toast. Our father doesn't like to be cold. He's always afraid we'll be cold. I'd like to help the Laframboise family not to be so cold. What can a child do? I have the impression, God, that You wanted children to be useless. We're always too young.

That's what I was thinking about when I looked towards the hill across from the church and saw our father's yellow sleigh-shed coming home, with the black horse and the white smoke. When I saw that, I decided that I could help the Laframboise family not to be so cold. I just had to wait for a while.

Our father led the horse into the stable. Then he went to tell the men in the general store about his trip. I watched the white smoke at the chimney of his sleigh-shed. It took a long time, but suddenly there wasn't any more. The fire was out. So then

I cooled down the camp-stove with snow. I wrenched it away from its chimney. I unscrewed its feet from the floor and I loaded it on my sleigh. It just looked like an empty barrel now.

I walked more than two miles. I went and knocked at the door of the Laframboise house and I said:

"I'm giving you our father's camp-stove; I don't know any camp-stove that makes so much heat."

The Laframboises didn't look as glad as I'd expected, but I don't think poor people need to be glad when you give them something. I was glad, though.

Can You explain it to me, God? Why did my father get mad? With his otter-skin cap, his coon-skin coat, his lined boots and his sheepskin vest, he doesn't need a camp-stove, too. The Laframboise family lives in a house where the wind comes in as if the door and the windows were open.

God, why was it a sin for me to try and make the Laframboise family not be so cold?

10

War Prayer

It's a good thing there's no war here in Canada, God! I wouldn't be able to come and pray to You in Your church, because You wouldn't have a church. There would be holes in the roof. The steeple would be broken off like a rotten tooth. The bricks would form the biggest pile in the village. Thank You, God, for not bringing a war to us. But I can't say thank You for making a war somewhere else.

It was in the newspaper: one and a half million adults and children were put to death in torture camps. I'm sure that wasn't Your work. It's the work of the Devil. But why didn't You stop the Devil from committing so much evil? One and a half million: 1,500,000. It's hard to write that number properly. I put down too many zeros, or not enough. That's a lot of children who were robbed of the lives You gave them. Your priest said in church: "They came into the world in sorrow, and they left it in sorrow, and they never knew the smile of joy." God, why didn't You stop the war?

The other day it said in the newspaper: "War to end in thirty-five days." Why do You have to wait for so many days? In fact, You've waited even longer. Much more than thirty-five days have passed, and the rain of fire continues. That was in the newspaper: "rain of fire." It isn't very good for the harvests. You are all-powerful, God. Send peace right away then, before another one and a half million children are burned in the torture camps.

Why didn't You send a wind of peace on the day the war started, when I was a tiny little child? I don't understand, God. War is like death, but a kind of death that hurts. Everything human beings do is something You invented. My head's too little to understand. If You are good, You can't have invented war. If You invented peace, You can't have invented war.

Fortunately, God, You seem to be helping the Allies win the war. In the paper the other day I saw an Allied tank just outside the Arc de Triomphe in Paris. The nun at school explained that the Arc de Triomphe is a monument in the very middle of France, like the hub of a wheel. I'd like to go to Paris, God, but not until the war is over. I wouldn't want the Nazis to throw a bomb at my rear end.

I heard on the radio that the Canadians have taken over Dieppe: some of them died, but the Nazis were scared of the ones that weren't dead. Our grandmother hopes our French Canadians don't swear too much. Their bad words would scandalize the French, who only know fancy words.

Then the Allies started going into Germany. Our mother keeps her turnips wrapped up in newspapers. If I unwrapped the turnips, I could read to You, God, what the newspaper says: "Allies wipe out Nazi detachment" or "3,000 (or 300,000, I don't remember which) Nazis taken prisoner every day"; "Stunning attack by Canadian troops heading for Ruhr and Rhineland." I don't know those places, but they were on maps in the newspaper.

Every day in the newspaper they show pictures of Canadian soldiers who died in the war. I suppose it doesn't hurt as much to die in the war as in a torture camp. When a soldier dies in the war he has a rifle and grenades or else a cannon. He can defend himself. Children in a torture camp can't kill three or four Nazis. They haven't eaten since last year. They're weak. Their legs and arms are as thin and dry as sticks of kindling. In the pictures, the dead Canadian soldiers have their caps in the proper place, on the side of their heads. Their cheeks are round. They all have a nice smile. They seem glad to be dying for their country. The ones that have been taken prisoner don't even have their hair mussed up. They look glad, too, as if somebody was tickling them with a feather to make them smile.

The newspaper said: "9,000 airplanes drop 14,000 bombs." All the planes had at least one bomb. Some of them had two. 5,000 airplanes had two bombs. Did 4,000 of the pilots forget to load their second bomb? War is complicated. Anyway, there was a "firestorm over Berlin."

It's sure the Canadians are going to win a victory in the old countries. I don't think the Nazis would have been able to start a war in Canada. In the summer there's too many mosquitoes and wasps. In the winter it's so cold the rifles would freeze. The enemies couldn't fire bullets in a blinding snowstorm when you can't see the sky or the Earth.

I wouldn't want to fight a war. Apparently, the Canadian soldiers like it. They go on a nice trip in a boat. Cigarettes don't cost much. Army boots are comfortable. We men really like to go hunting. Over there, the big game are the Nazis. In the old countries, girls and boys sleep in the same bed. Some Canadian soldiers like that, they said at the general store. Me, I wouldn't want to sleep in the same bed as a girl. I hate sleeping with my brother, and he's my own brother, so imagine sleeping with a girl from the old countries that I'd never seen in church. I wouldn't know what to say to her. In the bed, I wouldn't know which side to turn on.

The men in the general store said that far from here, in the place where Canada drops into the sea, there were fishermen fishing for fish. All of a sudden, they felt a big swell underneath. A huge wave, higher than any ordinary wave, shook their little boat. They saw bubbling like nobody had ever seen before. Then a gigantic boat surged out of the sea, ripping through the water, and it almost knocked the fishermen over. It was like a whale. It was a submarine dripping with water. A hatch opened. Men came out. With one hand, they beckoned the fishermen to come closer. In the other hand, they each held a machine gun. The fishermen were afraid. They shit in their rubber boots. Ever since then, they haven't wanted to get into their little boat again and go back to fish in the sea. I'd have been just as scared as they were.

All that the men with machine guns wanted was the fish in the bottom of the little boat. But they didn't know how to ask for the fish in our language. They talk a funny kind of talk that nobody around here's ever heard.

We can hear some funny kinds of talking on the radio when our father listens to the short-wave news from the old countries. God, You should have taught us how to understand the languages You invented. Our father and I wonder why the radio gives us news about the war in the old countries if we can't understand it. It's worse than not having any news.

Even though we're far away from the war, we have rationing on meat, sugar and flour. We suffer from the rationing, because we have to remember to take our ration books whenever we go to the general store. We often forget. The butcher doesn't want to collect the ration coupons: he doesn't know how to read and the coupons are covered with little writing. He says: "The Nazis won't lose the war any quicker if I collect those coupons." Apparently, rationing helps us send more food to our Canadian army and our Allies. In our village alone there's more cows than the old countries can eat, so we don't have to deprive ourselves. And as far as ration coupons are concerned, our father always has a pile of them in his pockets. People give them to him as a present when he goes travelling for his business. He often comes back with a bag of sugar or a sack of flour. War is sad, God.

When I was younger I saw the funeral of a dead man. He'd been killed in the war, far away. They didn't find all his pieces. Another soldier who hadn't been killed played the trumpet. It was so sad. I think the only person that wasn't bawling was the dead man.

At the general store, the men say the war's practically over. The soldiers who went to the old countries will be coming back to the village if they don't get killed. Thank You, God, if You end the war.

In our father's garage, You've seen it God, there's a big poster nailed to the wall. You remember, it shows Nazis with big caps on their heads and swastikas on their caps. They're standing there as stiff as Germans. They've got as many medals as a dog has fleas. All those Nazis are holding huge Nazi revolvers in their hands, powerful enough to kill a moose. All the Nazis have big smiles on their faces because they're aiming those revolvers at the little shaved heads of skinny children. The children haven't eaten for a long time. They look like skeletons, with only enough skin to hide their bones. They have hollow eyes; they're scared. They look like little dead children, but they're alive. God, make a miracle to stop all that suffering.

What good does it do to have children suffer? What good does it do You, God? Does it make You more perfect? Does it make the universe You created a finer place?

All those children have a star sewed to their shirts. If You want to make a miracle today, turn me into a soldier now. Don't wait for the next war. Make me a soldier right away. I'm ready to go right away; I'm ready to go right away to fight the war. I'm ready to take a rifle and go to countries like Germany, or even to Poland. There, I'd fight the war against the people who put those children in prison with a star on their shirts or their dresses.

Look, God, see how peaceful life is around Your church, with butterflies and wasps and cats and mosquitoes and cows. That's peace. Why don't You give the old countries the same peace and quiet?

I'm going to the rink. Please, God, don't forget me. I'd be really glad if Your holy finger could push the puck into the net, because on my own, without Your help, I'm not a very good hockey player.

11

Bum
Prayer

Is it because I'm the youngest, God, that I'm not allowed to see bums? When the others organize a bum-showing party, they don't want me to even show my face. I'd like to see bare bums too. I looked at mine in the big mirror in our parents' bedroom. Even if it hasn't got any hair on it, like the big kids said, I wouldn't be ashamed to show it to any girl in school, even the biggest girls in grade seven that put balls of wool in their blouses so people will think You've made them grow titties. Is it because I don't make as many mistakes in written dictations that they won't let me see their bums?

I really want to see some bare bums, God, like everybody else. I want to learn. All the big kids know how to play bum-showing, but I don't know the first thing about it. If they ever let me play I'd look like an idiot: I don't know the rules of the game. I'd feel pretty funny pulling down my pants in front of everybody and opening the trap door of my long-johns in front of the girls. I don't know about life, God. All I know is the responses and the questions in the catechism of Your religion as approved by the bishops of the diocese of Quebec. And the only other thing I know is how to conjugate regular and irregular verbs, the history of Canada with the Indians in bare bums and the French in lace petticoats and the exceptions to the plurals of words that end in "al." How do You expect me to be invited to play bum-showing, God, when I don't know anything else? In the middle of the bum-showing party I wouldn't know how to do anything but conjugate verbs that end in "eler" or "eter." Your catechism, the grammar approved by the Academy and the history of Canada as told by the Brothers of the Starched Bib are useless at a bum-showing party.

I can recite the grammatical rule for *amour, délice* and *orgue*, in the singular and the plural; I can declaim the rule for *gens* in the masculine and the feminine; but I don't know how to play bum-showing. Sometimes I wish I knew less about grammar and more about bums.

Anyway, I know where they play bum-showing. Last night I went to their hiding place, even though I wasn't invited. You know, God, how when the wind blows hard it drives all the snow up against Albert's hill, where the water reservoir is? Just in the fold of the hill, between where it's flat and where it starts to rise, the snow piles up. When there's only a little dusting of white snow everywhere else, in the fold of Albert's hill there's already a mountain of it. The wind drives the snow and makes it hard. So then, if you want to dig a cave, you just have to cut away some big blocks of snow. First you carve out the door, then you dig into the snow, one block at a time. It smells good. It smells clean. It smells of winter. It smells white. It smells like a good wind. As you go deeper, the room gets bigger and longer and wider; you smooth the walls, you smooth the ceiling. The snow is hard. Sounds are different. Voices aren't the same: it's like talking into cotton batting. The snow is light. It's as if we were cutting into the light. Sometimes the shovel hits ice: when that happens it's like finding a bone in the light. Then the floor turns hard because it's been walked on so much. The snow is packed so hard it's almost ice. It's as clean as a freshly waxed floor. And the ceiling is solid: it's made round like the Eskimos' igloos.

And it smells so good in the cave: the good smell of ice. It's mild, so mild it almost seems warm. You're protected in there like mice in a fresh loaf of white homemade bread.

When it's all finished, when the walls of the cave and the ceilings are nice and even, nice and smooth, a wall made out of big blocks of snow goes up outside the entrance for protection from the wind and from any enemies that might attack. It's there, inside the cave, that they play bum-showing. They let me help them dig the cave, but then they wouldn't let me play. It isn't fair. If I'm allowed to dig with them, God, they ought to let me play bum-showing with them.

They said: "You're too young, you can't play with us." Even though I'm young, I really want to see some girls' bums. Not like my sisters'. Real girls' bums, of the girls in higher grades.

I have as much right to play bum-showing as they do. I may be younger but I have a bum too. I'm at the same page as them in grammar and arithmetic and catechism and sacred history. Do they expect me to wait till I'm in the next grade to play bum-showing? *They* aren't waiting.

Maybe their parties aren't that much fun. Bums, bums: they're skin, just like feet. I don't know anybody that puts on feet-showing parties. Actually, God, what I'd really be curious to see again is titties. I think titties are a lot more interesting than bums. But I'll have to wait for the higher grades because the girls in our class haven't got any more titties than I do.

They're scared, apparently, that if I play with them I'll tell everybody about their parties. I'd be way too embarrassed for that. It's something I'd never tell anybody. Those aren't things you talk about. Bum-showing sounds like fun to play, not to talk about.

They think all I'm good for is delivering the secret notes they write and pass around when the nun's at the blackboard with her back turned.

You know Robert, he's the leader of the bum-showing party. He's a big boy and he sits right behind me. When the nun was writing a problem in long-division on the blackboard, Robert dropped some notes on my desk, all folded over so nobody could read what was in them. Every note had a name on it, just like a letter. There was one for Liliane, one for Irene, one for Lucette, one for Guy and one for Honoré's boy. I couldn't read what was written inside, but I could guess. So I turned around and I said to Robert:

"I want to play bum-showing with the rest of you."

Robert insulted me as if I was the size of a prune. He said to me:

"Wait till your belly-button's dry."

I want to play bum-showing like everybody else, God. So, like it says in the books that belong to the Brothers of the Bib, I retorted:

"My belly-button's just as dry as yours is."

"You haven't got a beard on your chin. A child can't play bum-showing till he's got hair."

The others around Robert burst out laughing. I could tell they were making fun of me.

The nun turned around. She got down off her platform and walked towards us. I had just enough time to snatch the notes from Robert and stuff them in the pocket of my pants. She didn't see a thing. Since there was nothing to see, she went back to the blackboard. And I asked permission to pee because I wanted to read the little notes.

It's written on the wall of the crapper that You can see us. I can't believe, God, that You spend Your time watching schoolchildren piss and do the other thing that's good for your health even if you have to swallow castor oil to do it. But if You did look at me, You know what I did: I read Robert's notes. And every one said the same thing: "Theirs a bumm-showing partey after Vesters tonihgt." When I read that, I thought: bums make you forget how to spell.

I went back to the classroom with that look on my face as if I'd pissed for too long to have had enough time to read the notes, and I handed them around to the people they were addressed to.

I went to church, to Vespers. It was the longest Vespers I ever heard. I knew I wasn't going to play bum-showing, but I looked at Robert and Guy and Honoré's boy and Lucette and Irene and Liliane, and they kept turning around to each other, and I could tell they weren't thinking about You, but about their party. Even me, I didn't think of You: I was only thinking about their bum-showing party. I wasn't invited.

When the priest sang his last note, the bum-showing party team was already outside. I was one of the last ones out, along with the old people who seem to think that religious services are never long enough. I didn't want to be seen.

The night was a beautiful blue with hundreds of millions of stars. The snow was beautiful and white. Because of the cold and the wind, it was hard, and it creaked under the soles of my boots. It was already night, but at night there's often a kind of dark brightness. Instead of going along the street to our house, I turned into the field, towards the water reservoir, towards Albert's hill where the cave had been dug out of the snow.

I saw from a distance that there was already a spot of light where the cave was. They'd already lit the candles. I could see the light through the snow. I thought: "If they've made a light it means they've already started playing bum-showing."

So I approached, as wily as a real Iroquois. Instead of heading for the door of the cave, which was certainly being guarded while the others were busy showing each other their bums, I made my way to the top of the cave, towards the top of the snowbank where the cave was dug. And then I started to crawl like a real warrior. And soon I could see the light of the candles through the roof of snow. I thought:

"I'll stop. They're here, underneath. So if I dig myself a little hole here, I should be able to see some bums right now."

Then I opened my hand in my mitten and I stuck it in the snow. I started digging a nice little hole in the roof to spy on them. I kept turning my hand like our grandfather's bit-brace. Without a sound, very softly, I dug. My arm went deeper and deeper into the roof. Suddenly, I'd dug right through it. And I fell into the hole as if You'd pulled the Earth out from under me.

The roof of the cave collapsed. I heard shouting. I shouted too. I landed on somebody but I don't know who, because everything was covered with snow. What shouting! By stepping on legs and heads, which I could feel under my boots, I pulled myself up, but I couldn't see anything except the beautiful bright night and a big hole in the snow. Inside, though, there was all kinds of whimpering. Very slowly the snow at the bottom of the hole began to move and I saw heads and arms emerge, I saw bodies straighten up, and everybody was complaining that their bums were cold. They started looking in the snow for their pants and skirts. It took some of them ten or fifteen minutes to find theirs. They didn't even notice I was there. What they were saying wasn't prayers.

The snow was slowly melting on the skin of their bums and God, I'll never see as many as I saw on Sunday night. I saw, but I didn't play. I'm going to grow up, and I'll let You know about *my* first party.

Goodbye. Thank You, God, for letting me see some bare bums! I'm running to school now. I can't wait to find out if the bum team's organizing another party.

12

Funeral
Prayer

I really like it, God, when someone dies; I come and help our grandfather, who's the sexton at the church. But You shouldn't make children die. Because children are made for life, not for death. There are plenty of old people who've been sick a long time who'd like to go and see You. Invite them, God, but what use can a child my age be in Heaven? Ask any child with skates under his feet, ask him if he'd prefer Earth or Heaven. At our age, we prefer Earth — except for people who think they're angels and act as if they haven't got an asshole.

I'd rather be alive than dead today. I'd rather be in Your church than in Your Heaven. I'm glad You took Ginette's life instead of mine. Ginette only wanted to play. You shouldn't have made her die. It doesn't make sense. We've just come into the world. Do we have to leave already? You shouldn't give us life just to take it away from us. We'll never see Ginette again.

I'd like to know the explanation. You take Ginette away from us, whose life hasn't begun yet, and You leave us old Ephremette Duclos, who must be at least a hundred and three or a hundred and four. She's afraid You've forgotten her here on Earth. She thinks she'll never see Your Heaven.

Ginette came first in class, after Martine and Aline. She hardly ever made mistakes in dictation. Big Red made forty-eight mistakes in a ten- or eleven-line dictation. The nun at school said that he murders the French language. And besides, Big Red can't even multiply nine-sevens-are-sixty-three; he always gets it mixed up with eight-sevens-are-fifty-six. And besides, he uses rude words, so rudely rude I can't repeat them in Your church. If You heard them, You'd blush as red as a hen's ass. "God plucked Ginette like a little wildflower": that's what the nun told us. So I said: "A little wildflower will grow back, but Ginette won't." The nun replied: "Ginette won't grow back like a little earthly flower, but like a little celestial flower, in Heaven." And just then, the nun's tears overflowed her eyes. She wiped them with her big starched handkerchief and she sniffed.

She was so sad, the nun. If she was so sure that she'd see our little flower in Heaven she wouldn't have cried so bitterly. God, You should have come and taken old Ephremette Duclos: she's all wrinkled like an old apple that froze on the tree. It would smooth out her face to have it flower again up in Heaven.

Why Ginette? Her parents have hardly any children: four or five. Why didn't you pluck a child from a family with sixteen or fifteen? Anyway, I'm glad you took Ginette and not me. I'd be curious to see Heaven, but before You invite me to move, God, give me the chance to see a little of Earth. When I've seen it long enough, perhaps I'll understand why You invented death.

I'll never live long enough to understand why Ginette died. Perhaps it's only in Heaven that we can understand death. It can't be something bad — You created it: like life, like birds and trout and horses. Killing someone is a sin. God, why did You kill Ginette?

I'm with our grandfather the sexton. We're decorating the church for Ginette's funeral. The whole school will come. We have to make the church beautiful and sad. I think Ginette will like her funeral. The church will be blacker than it's ever been: it's very, very sad. The church seems more like a big tent made of black mourning. I've heard the choir practising their song. The *Dies irae* will squeeze out so many tears, people will wonder if the whole school has peed on the floor.

We get a day off school because Ginette died; at least she didn't die for nothing. At home, Imelda has a toothache. Imelda's the maid who came in to help our mother. She's crying because she has a toothache; she whimpers like a dog with a belly-ache. It's a wisdom tooth.

This is the day the dentist comes to the village to pull out all the aching teeth. He comes on the first Friday of the month. Until then, toothaches have to be endured. We must endure our toothaches with patience. On the dentist's day, the people

119

Funeral
Prayer

with toothaches squeal like pigs at the slaughter-house. I cried, too, when our grandmother tied a piece of thread for sewing our grandfather's trouser buttons around one of my teeth. She pulled hard enough to make my head come unstuck. On the dentist's Friday, you can see red patches every-where. The dentist's victims spit blood wherever they go.

Imelda, our maid, has heard the squealing, she's seen the tooth-blood all over the village and she's as scared as if she was going to die.

I hope Ginette didn't have time to be scared. The accident happened so fast she didn't see it coming. Afterwards, she was asleep. I hope death didn't come to her like a nightmare. God, I hope that besides making a child die You didn't scare her, too. I'm sorry, but I don't understand. Anyway, it's no sin not to understand. I'm just trying to understand life, God, but You don't give many explanations. The nun at school doesn't under-stand much more than I do. Just between us, God, do You understand?

Our father said to Imelda, to console her:

"Don't be scared, Imelda — it won't hurt as much as marriage."

Imelda's a mother because she had a baby. She's no more than fourteen years old. Our mother said it was a scandal to have a baby at an age when you should be in school. Our father said she was too young to know what she was doing. Our mother told him that when you do those things you know what you're doing. I didn't understand that either. God, I'm really fed up with not understanding. Did You put me on Earth just to understand nothing?

Imelda was in her room. She was shrieking through the door that she wasn't going out to let the dentist torture her gums. She said she preferred the pain of her tooth to the pain of the pliers. Our mother shouted at her through the door to come out and drink a nice glass of warm milk. Our father shouted through the door that if she didn't leave her room he'd go and get the dentist, and that if the dentist didn't want to come he'd borrow a pair of pliers from Monsieur Juste, the blacksmith, the ones he uses for pulling nails out of horseshoes. Our mother said through the door that Imelda shouldn't be afraid of the dentist who was going to take away her pain. Our father added:

"If you wait, Imelda, you won't have just one rotten tooth, you'll have a mouthful. Your teeth will look like a row of rotten cherries. And it's not just your teeth that will rot if you wait, your whole jaw will, and even your spine, and then you'll never find a husband."

Then our mother shouted at our father: "This is no time to be talking about a husband to that child with an aching tooth." Our father replied, shouting through the door: "And I say that if she'd had a husband she wouldn't have put her baby in the orphanage." Our mother replied: "This is no time to be talking about that — she has a toothache." Our father replied: "If she's got a toothache, she should go to the dentist." So then our mother said: "Imelda's afraid of the dentist, and if you keep yelling like that, she'll be afraid of you!" So then our father punched the door with his fist: "If Imelda wants a toothache let her keep her tooth-ache. And I'll shout as loud as I want because this is my house and I've almost finished paying off the mortgage." Our mother tried to calm him down: "Imelda's so young." Our father shouted as loud as before: "She was old enough to get stuck with a baby." Our mother was taking Imelda's side: "She's gone through so many trials." Our father concluded: "Imelda's gone wherever she felt like going. . . . What she needs is tin pants, like a can of peas." So then our mother shook her head and she was almost white: "I never would have married you if I'd known you talked like that." So then our father decided to go outside for a breath of air, but not before he asked: "Will you tell me why Imelda wanted to have a toothache?"

And that's what happened. When they were done, they'd just start all over again. Our father stayed in the house today because he had a bad cough.

I don't know if Imelda went to see the dentist, but our father laid down the law. He said: "I'm not paying for a servant with one cheek bigger than her head because she won't have a little baby-tooth pulled out. I don't have much hope for the younger generation."

It's quieter in here, God, in Your church. Our grandfather the sexton and me, we're getting ready for Ginette's funeral. It's sad but it's happy. We're hanging big mourning curtains at the windows. To fasten them up at the top we use a pole that must be twenty feet high, or twenty-two. When I run with it through the church, the wings of the curtains spread open and float in the air. It looks like a big black butterfly. Excuse me, God, but I run from one end of Your church to the other and our grandfather the sexton lets me. . . . He doesn't stop me, he just watches me and smiles. . . . I haven't often seen our grandfather smile. If I was an angel in paradise, God, You wouldn't stop me from running or from flying with my little angel's wings. Our grandfather the sexton watches me running, but he must be thinking about Ginette who'll never run again.

You see everything in the whole universe, God. You must have seen her fall on the ice. We'd made an ice slide in the schoolyard. We run and run, as fast as we can, and then we slide on our boots as far as possible. Ginette fell, her feet shot up higher than her head, and her head hit the ice. Why did

Ginette lose her footing? She'd slid a hundred times before she fell. We didn't see anything, just the blood pouring from her nose. Apparently, Ginette's head was shattered like an egg.

Nothing happens on Earth except through Your holy will. God, I can't believe that You pushed Ginette.

I'd rather be in my shoes. I wouldn't want to feel dead and to know I was going to be buried six feet under the ground. Instead of being in Ginette's coffin I'd rather be in our house, listening to our father and our mother and Imelda fight; I'd rather hear Imelda screaming in the dentist's chair when the pliers are in her mouth.

If it wasn't for Ginette's death, I wouldn't be helping our grandfather prepare for a funeral. Ginette's funeral will be a nice one. We've hung black banners on the walls. We've draped black veils over the statues. We've covered the windows with black curtains. We've hooked black pennants in the ceilings and they fall down onto the walls. We've tied black ribbons to the crucifix of the death of Christ. I like to help our grandfather the sexton when we unwind curtains or banners that are as long as the road from our village to the next one. We're going to decorate all the pews in the church with black bows. In a while I'll take out the priest's black chasuble. Ginette's entitled to all the official sadness.

Thank You God for not pushing me on the ice. Thank You God for keeping me alive. I hope You're going to invite Ginette into Your Heaven. I have to stop running from one end of the church to the other, holding the pole at arm's length and the two black curtain wings that float in the air. Our grandfather the sexton's calling because he needs me for the catafalque. I think the catafalque's the most beautiful thing of all, all black with gilt decorations and big painted wood candles. It's as beautiful as a hearse, even though it hasn't got wheels or a horse.

When the catafalque's all set up, I like going underneath it, where the coffin will be. I stand there in the dark for a long time, without opening the velvet curtains. I'm practising for when I'm dead. God, I'd rather live!

13

Bread
Prayer

I haven't come to see You for a long time, God. It's been a long time since I've committed a sin. I'm going to confess an old one. It's a mortal sin, I think. A big sin, but I was only little. I didn't go to church yet. I was too little.

There are so many mysteries in life. You shouldn't have created so many mysteries, God, or else you should have given us more intelligence. I've tried to understand the mystery of the bread that's blessed by the priest and is changed into the flesh of Jesus, as the catechism says. Oh, I eat it, but just between us, it doesn't have much meat. But I prefer it that way. Eating little bits of Jesus isn't the most appetizing thing I can think of. Good thing it's a mystery. I'd rather eat bread-and-maple-butter than bread-and-the-body-of-Jesus.

The nun at school told us that savage Indians ate a number of French missionaries, young ones and old ones. We aren't savage Indians. So what does that make us if we eat the flesh of Jesus? You see, God, every time I ask a question I get another mystery for an answer. I'm going to confess my old sin.

One Sunday our mother was putting on her fur coat for Sundays. I said:

"Me too, I want to go to Mass."

Our mother looked at our father. Our father looked at our mother. Both of them looked as proud as they did when they realized I didn't need a diaper any more. Our mother said:

"So young, and already so pious! He'll be our family's little priest."

"If he's that pious I won't be able to count on him to take over the business. We'll have to make another one."

That's what he said. Those very words. I didn't understand what he meant, but I wasn't worried. It's not until you have a beard that you understand everything. But then you shave it. I'd like You to tell me when it is that girls understand. They never get beards. Except if they turn into old nuns.

That Sunday I was just little, and our father said:

"Since this one likes to pray to God, let's take advantage of it before he changes his mind!"

So then my mother dressed me up in my white rabbit-fur bonnet and my coat with the white rabbit-fur collar; she put my white boots on my feet, pulled on my blue leggings, bundled me up in my white wool muffler as long as from here to the American border, and then she put my hands in three pairs of mittens. Our mother and our father carried me to the church. I've never seen them so proud. I didn't cry and I wanted to pray to You.

"How do you manage to keep him from crying?" asked the ladies. "The first time we brought ours to church they made such a racket — real little devils, terrified of the holy water. They wanted to run away from the church like little godless Communists – or the damned. God bless them!"

"This one," said our mother, "has always had an instinct for religious things. I'm not lying: look at those blue eyes of his, like a reflection of the Virgin

Mary's robe. This child — I'm not lying, Madame — this child looks up to Heaven more than he looks down to Earth."

"If you walk with your nose in the air for too long, you sometimes fall down the cellar stairs," said our father. "Wife, we're taking our boy to Mass, not to his canonization!"

I'd never seen so many people sitting down. Nobody looked anybody else in the eye. They were all looking at the backs of heads. Nobody dared to talk. The only thing that was moving was the little flame at the tip of the candles. And the coughing in there sounded like an engine that doesn't want to start. God, it was so boring. Your priest said the other day that the Mass is the closest thing in life to Heaven. Your life must be really dull, God! If Your angels sing like our choir, a person might as well be listening to cats in heat. I said very loud — well, not all that loud but since everybody was asleep with their eyes open it seemed loud:

"*Maman*, I want to go home!"

Our mother plastered her hand over my mouth. She practically suffocated me to shut me up.

Everybody turned their heads toward me. All those eyes staring at me were reproaching me for something. I started to howl. It was no louder under Your sky when the atomic bomb exploded. The faces of the men turned to the front again. The faces of the women stayed turned in my direction, giving me lovely melting smiles or blowing little kisses. They were trying to soften me up so I'd stop crying. I wanted to leave. I was too little to drag our mother and father away. All I could do was howl.

Suddenly our mother said:

"Look at Monsieur le curé."

First of all, he didn't look like a monsieur. He was wearing a dress. He was all decorated like a bride. Suddenly I noticed I'd stopped crying. The people were awake now. They were standing, sitting, kneeling. They were doing gymnastics like in school. The priest was talking to them. Sometimes they didn't answer. Other times they mumbled something. God, have You ever gone to Mass? There's nothing longer. The organ was purring. I couldn't help it. I fell asleep.

Our mother knows more things than we do, but she doesn't like that. She wants us to know as much as she does. She's always trying to teach us. So there she is, shaking me.

"Wake up! You mustn't sleep in the Lord's house. . . . "

Don't You ever sleep in Heaven? When our father doesn't sleep he gets in a bad mood. I hope You sleep. I know that You rest on Sunday. The nun at school said so. Our father rests on Sunday, too. So does our grandfather. They snore as soon as their eyes are shut. Do You snore like our father and our grandfather? I guess not. It would make a sky-quake. You probably snore silently.

By now I was awake, but our mother kept on jabbing me with her elbow. She was shaking me like a bottle of medicine. She was showing me something up in the choir, pointing with her finger. All I could see was the priest in his bride's dress. I could see the altar boys, wearing skirts like girls. I could see Jesus nailed to the cross, looking as if he'd like to fold his arms. I could see a lot of lighted candles and a lot of shiny things that were giving off a lot of smoke that smelled nice. Our mother kept shaking me and saying the same thing over and over:

"Wake up! Monsieur le curé's going to hold up the baby Jesus."

"Did Monsieur le curé have a baby?"

That was worth opening my eyes for, but I didn't see anything very interesting. The priest was standing high up, at the altar. An altar boy in a surplice was waving the censer that was smoking as much as our father, but it didn't stink as bad. Another one had got hold of a little bell. He wanted to ring it but he didn't have permission. On the altar was the biggest book I'd ever seen in my life. Then hundreds of candles were lit. I asked our mother:

"Where's the baby Jesus?"

"Look carefully!" she whispered. "You'll see."

She lifted me up so I could stand on the kneeling bench. It wasn't high enough: all I could see was a lot of coats with a lot of belts.

"I can't see anything!" I whimpered.

She helped me climb onto the pew.

Above the altar, on the big crucifix, with his arms stretched out and his hands nailed down, Christ looked as if he couldn't think of what to say. A sunbeam was shining on the big crucifix, exactly like in the pictures the nun gives us in school.

"I can't see baby Jesus!" I yelled.

Our mother smiled submissively. She didn't say anything, because church is a place where you don't talk to anybody, except You, God. Still, I could hear the words she wasn't saying to the other ladies:

"It isn't easy to bring up children nowadays, Madame."

"I don't know what they've got in their blood, Madame, but you can tell when they're still very young that they don't like religion."

"Oh, Madame, mine already knows the responses to the catechism by heart."

I'd decided to leave.

"I want to go out and play!"

Our mother, disheartened, took me in her arms. She held me against her and whispered in my ear:

"The priest is preparing the bread. When the

bread is ready, the priest will pray to God. And then there'll be the miracle of the Mass. The bread will be changed into baby Jesus."

"Like magic?"

"In church, magic is called a miracle. Repeat that after me: mir-a-cle . . . "

"I can't see baby Jesus!"

"Wait, the priest is preparing the bread."

He was very busy doing something.

"When will we see the magic of baby Jesus?"

My mother whispered in my ear:

"Religion takes patience, dear. Look. Wait. Believe."

The priest's arms unfolded and folded and the maniple on his arm went flying in every direction. He was moving the way our mother moves when she's kneading bread. I often watched our mother sprinkle flour on her ball of dough, then punch it like a boxer until it was flat and she could shape it into a ball again.

Finally, I figured it out. The priest, I thought, is kneading the dough, and he's going to make us a little baby Jesus out of bread dough.

My mother was glad to see that I'd calmed down. She continued to explain the miracle of the Mass.

"The bread will be ready soon. And then, with his prayers, the priest will change the bread into a wonderful baby Jesus. This will be the first time you've seen the miracle. When the altar boy rings his bell, you must kneel; the priest will hold up the baby Jesus in his arms to show us. When you see him, you must bow your head. You'll remember this moment all your life. It's the good Lord himself that you will see."

Your priest stopped waving his arms around. He'd finished kneading his bread. Then he bowed his head to recite some prayers. And then all of a sudden the altar boy tinkled his bell.

I was expecting to see the baby Jesus. I'd seen a few babies in my life. I knew what a baby looked like, but I'd never seen the baby Jesus.

Our mother said:

"Adore the baby Jesus!"

I couldn't see anything. I looked again. What did I see in the priest's hands? Nothing. A little white ball. Not even a ball. Something flat. No bigger than a quarter. It didn't have a fuzzy head. It didn't have arms or legs. It didn't even have a diaper. It wasn't a baby. And if it wasn't a baby, it couldn't be the baby Jesus!

I protested as loud as I could:

"That's no baby Jesus!"

Our mother clamped her hand over my mouth, and there was nothing gentle about it this time. I howled in disappointment:

"That isn't Jesus!"

Our mother tried to pacify me.

"It isn't Jesus!"

"Child, you have to believe in religion."

I replied:

"That isn't the baby Jesus!"

At first everybody was facing us, but they turned around in a hurry. Nobody wanted to hear the blasphemy of someone possessed by the demon so young.

"That isn't Jesus! There's no miracle!"

Our mother was disheartened. Our father was ashamed of the little monster who was his son.

Our mother couldn't control me. She ordered our father:

"Get your little Communist out of here!"

God, I don't know if You've listened to my whole story right to the end. It's an old sin of disbelief that I wanted to confess to You today. I'm glad I thought of that one. I'd forgotten it. I pray for Your forgiveness.

God, I believe in the mysteries and the miracles of Your religion; I believe in everything. But just between us, I've never in my life seen a baby that's all flat and white like a communion wafer.

14

Spanking
Prayer

God, do You remember the first time Your mother spanked You? When I'm as old as an ancestor, when I'm forty or even fifty, I'll still remember the first time I was punished.

I'll never, ever forget it. I was thinking about my spanking today, because I saw the youngest of the nineteen Lamontagnes being educated by his mother while his father was in the general store with my father. If it's true, God, that we learn through our backsides what our heads don't want to take in, the Lamontagne kid's going to know as much as Your priest.

Getting back to my own hiding, my mother's hand must still be printed on my backside, even though I was wearing my fleece-lined winter underwear and my heavy winter pants.

I was punished because I went sliding in my sleigh. That's all. A slide in the quiet snow. Everything was peaceful. There was only one horse in the village. He was quiet. There was nothing but the quiet street. Quiet snow. Nobody in the street. The smoke from the chimneys didn't make a sound. There were no birds cheeping. It was like in my reader: "The snow had spread its white mantle of silence." I was the only child outside. So quiet. I was alone in the street. There was only one horse in the village. Nothing happened. The last time our mother lit into me, it was because nothing happened. The blows landed on my rear end like the bomb on Japan. Maybe I got punished because something could have happened. A child's sleigh, a quiet horse beside the general store, a main street, fresh snow with no horse buns: what could happen?

Today I saw the youngest of the nineteen Lamontagnes get his backside warmed. He squealed like a pig at the slaughterhouse. I remembered, God, that I'd never told You about my first spanking. It was an important stage in my life. Before your first spanking, you're a child; after it, you're a man. Your first spanking marks your true birth. I got mine because, on that day, nothing happened.

It was a quiet, peaceful day; I've never seen such a quiet day. Nothing happened. No baby arrived. No pig was squealing because his artery was being sliced. No man from the Beauce passed through our village of Dorchester. The only event that was worthy of note was my spanking.

Our mother had said to me:

"The snow is lovely, the village is peaceful, it's not too cold — go outside and play so you'll have nice pink lungs and rosy cheeks."

And then she bundled me up. She swaddled me in layers and layers of wool and cloth. Our mother has a lot of intuition. She knew she was going to be giving me a spanking. She wanted to protect my rear end with layers of wool. She put on my good white rabbit-skin cap. I was dressed just like a real baby. I think I actually was one. I was wearing a diaper because when I sat down outside in the cold snow, it gave me ideas and I peed, I couldn't help it. You know what it's like, God, when you're two years old. Besides that, I had my wool muffler wound around my head a dozen times to protect me from the wind. My clothes were like the armour of a deep-sea diver twenty thousand leagues under the sea. There's a book called that at school but the nun won't lend it to me until I'm thirteen. When you're that old, you have a beard and you don't read books because you're chasing girls.

So our mother said as she opened the door:

"Remember now, don't cross the street."

I understood. She wanted me to play. She said it again:

"Don't cross the street. It's dangerous to cross the street, very dangerous."

There's only one street here, but in town there are lots of streets; towns are full of streets. If it's so dangerous to cross a street, I don't imagine there are very many children left in those towns.

"*Maman* says not cross street; me not cross street, I promise."

It was beautiful. You had given us a beautiful day, all painted blue and white. If one of Your angels had flown by, we would have heard the feathers in his wings brushing against the air of the sky. Nothing was stirring: not a cat, not a dog, not a bird, not one old person. The smoke almost writhed as it came out of the chimneys. For the day to be so quiet and peaceful, everything would have to be dead.

I looked towards the bottom of the hill; the hills looked as if they were part of the white sky. I raised my eyes to see the sky; to me it looked like blue snow. The air smelled of the maple wood that burned in our stoves.

In those days houses weren't coloured. Their old grey wood looked as if it had floated in the lake, but the houses had only floated through time.

Between the two rows of houses, the village street went way down to the bottom of the hill, way past the end of the village. If you climbed up, it passed in front of the church, but it also went even farther, because it came back down again. There wasn't one horse on the road, or a sleigh, or a person, or a bird, or a horse bun with birds pecking at it.

Our oldest brother had a wonderful sleigh. It was planted in the snow. Once I went sliding down hill with our oldest brother. We'd climbed up till we were across from the church, and then we'd come back down the hill. It was as fast as falling. It made a wind that slapped you in the face and made your eyes cry. The wind froze my nose, even though I was hidden behind our brother's head. It was fun. Afterwards, he didn't want to slide down hill with me again. He said that I weighed too much and that the sleigh didn't slide fast enough. I wanted to go again. Our oldest brother ran away with the big boys.

And that day I saw the sleigh. Our brother wasn't there. It had pretty red drawings on it, our brother's sleigh. I decided to borrow it.

So I pulled the sleigh behind me. I was all alone in the street with our brother's sleigh. The snow had piled up and the street was almost as high as the roofs of the houses. (I didn't measure it with our grandfather's folding ruler.) I climbed with our oldest brother's sleigh all the way up till I was across from the church, on the back of the hill. And I didn't cross the street.

So then I sat in the sleigh, and it started to zoom down the hill. It went a lot faster than when our oldest brother had gone sliding with me. It was like flying, but with kicks in the rear end because of the bumps. I had tears in my eyes and ice on my eyelashes. It was so much fun that I was laughing very loud; perhaps I was crying. I was alone on the street and I was sliding down hill like the big children. I hadn't crossed to the other side of the street.

I was obeying our mother's commandment, God, but Bissonnette's horse crossed the street.

Bissonnette's horse was outside the general store because Bissonnette was inside the store buying things. When he finished his shopping, Bissonnette told his horse to cross the street to go where he was going.

There I was, shooting down the hill like a lightning bolt of wool and fur, on our brother's sleigh. Just then, Bissonnette's horse was crossing the street. He was pulling a sleigh loaded with white birch logs. I was in our brother's sleigh, going like the wind. Bissonnette's horse was right in front of me, and he was in no hurry. His sleigh seemed not to be moving because the logs were so heavy. I was

145

Spanking
Prayer

laughing too hard, or crying, and I thought: I'm going to run into the sleigh-load of logs. I was laughing too hard — or crying too hard — to stop. I was travelling too fast to stop. Just when I thought I was going to crash into the logs, our oldest brother's sleigh decided to slip between Bissonnette's horse's legs. Me and the sleigh passed between the horse's two front legs and his two hind legs. And I kept going. The sleigh wasn't going quite so fast, but I was laughing, or maybe crying, even harder.

Nothing happened. But our grandmother saw me zip past under Bissonnette's horse. She came out in just a dress, with no coat or boots, wearing her shoes in the winter snow. She was crying, not laughing. She caught me with one hand, and with the other she grabbed hold of the sleigh and, as fast as I'd come down the hill, she took me up to the house and told our mother that she'd seen the horse cross the street and that she'd seen me crossing underneath the horse.

That was all she said. I'm going now, God, because I wouldn't want to commit the sin of being late for school.

But our mother, I've never seen her as mad as she was on the day of my first spanking, which was the hardest ever known in the western hemisphere.

I hadn't crossed the street. Our mother was giving me slaps and kisses. They felt the same to me.

Spanking
Prayer

15

Prayer
for the City
of Quebec

Do You recognize me, God? It's me, Your little boy.
Did You recognize me at first glance? Have I
changed? Before, I'd never seen the City of
Quebec. Today, I'm *in* the City of Quebec. Have I
turned into a braggart like everybody else in the
City of Quebec? I wouldn't want to insult You,
God, but look at me: I'm going to make my face
look like a person from Quebec. Is it boastful
enough? I just want to show You. Excuse me. If I
stick my nose up as if everything smelled bad I'd
look even more like a Quebecker. There are a lot of
Quebeckers. The City of Quebec is full of them.
They overflow into the countryside.

Before, I'd never been to Quebec. In case You
don't recognize me now that I look like a Quebecker, God, I should tell You that I'm Your little

boy from the village who often goes to the church to pray to You.

There's a great big huge church here. It's the first time I've come to see You in a foreign church. You seem different in this church in Quebec. I hope You haven't turned boastful like the Quebeckers. It feels funny. As if I was going to see our mother in another house. In Quebec, God, You seem foreign. I'm sorry.

When our Uncle Phidyme parked his car in front of the church so he could go into a bank with some papers he'd taken from his safe, I decided to come in and pray to You for a while. It's a good thing You're everywhere at once; people like me who travel can find You everywhere.

It's a nice church You've got here. Our church in the village could fit inside it several times. I see gold everywhere, gilding everywhere, on the altar, the ceiling, the columns. According to the nun at school, You were born with Your bum in the straw. I wasn't there but . . . if You were born in a stable with the oxen and the sheep, You must be proud to have so much gold. All that gold, those thousand candles burning in front of the statues, all those vigil lights: either Quebeckers are really pious or else they're hypocrites.

Our oldest brother stayed in the machine waiting for our uncle. He got behind the wheel and pretended he was driving. He wants to look interesting to the Quebec girls. I don't like the Quebec girls, they walk around as if they haven't let a fart in three months. When I'm grown up, I'm going to get married in our church, to a girl who You made from our village. Unless I go and marry a girl who wears a mask and rides a camel in Arabia.

Our brother came to Quebec once before, for his tonsils. He had them pulled out at the hospital in Quebec. You didn't give me tonsils so I didn't think I'd ever see Quebec.

Quebec, You know, was founded by Samuel de Champlain in 1608, on Cap Diamant, which was discovered by Captain Jacques Cartier in 1534. It has the Château Frontenac. Frontenac was a governor of New France. In 1690 he told the English: "I have no reply to make to your general other than from the mouths of my cannon." The City of Quebec was taken by the English in 1759, at the

Battle of the Plains of Abraham, which still isn't over today. The nun at school told us that. There's a stone wall all around Quebec, but it didn't keep out the English. A bridge stretches across the St Lawrence River to get to Quebec. It collapsed twice: once in 1907 and once in 1916. It didn't collapse a third time or we'd have known about it. Today, machines drive over the bridge, and big trucks loaded with logs and even trains. I wouldn't be surprised if it collapsed again. Jacques Cartier thought that Cap Diamant was a real diamond. Maybe Jacques Cartier needed eyeglasses, which were invented by a monk in the Middle Ages. In Quebec, there are lots of boats in the harbour. You can cross the St Lawrence River in a boat, too. Quebec is the city of Monsieur Duplessis, the Prime Minister. Our father says that if Monsieur Duplessis was the Prime Minister of the whole world there wouldn't be a war. In Quebec there's also the Cardinal who forbids people to commit the sin of dancing. And there are big department stores where the loggers go to spend a little money when they come down from the North in the spring. Besides that, I know the Quebec Aces who play hockey and aren't nearly as good as Maurice Richard's Canadiens. Then there's seminaries where they grow. And most of all, there's the world wrestling champions who come to Quebec to fight. I know lots of things today that I didn't know before I came to Quebec. We passed the brothels on rue Saint-Paul.

Our Uncle Phidyme told us those houses are full of girls who tickle you. I don't like being tickled. Uncle Phidyme had a paper to be signed for his business in an office on rue Saint-Paul. He told us to wait in his machine. We waited. When he came out of the special office he seemed really happy. I think he'd worked out his business the way he wanted. Anyway, he was in a good mood and he was singing:

Grand-maman, ah oui grand-maman,
Vous avez dû passer par là!

The people in the office seemed to be polite. When we started off in the machine a pretty employee at the window, wearing a lot of lipstick, blew kisses to our Uncle Phidyme. And the people in the office had perfumed him with strong perfume.

Oh, there are such big houses in Quebec! But none of them are high enough to scrape the sky. Now that I've seen the City of Quebec with my own eyes, God, I'm going to say a prayer of thanks to You for letting me see what so many people in the world have never seen. And I'm going to say a prayer to ask You to show me New York some day. Please, God, hold my hand to guide me in New York and in Paris and in the land of a Thousand and One Nights and in Jerusalem and Rome and all the wonderful countries I see pictures of in the *Encyclopédie des pays et nations*.

Anyway, thank You for giving our Uncle Phidyme the inspiration to take us with him to the City of Quebec. When I'm an old man, I still won't forget this wonderful day in my life. I'll still be talking about this trip when I'm as old as forty or even fifty, if You haven't taken away the breath You gave me when You gave me life.

In the village we were playing; we'd hooked up a telephone with sewing thread and two empty tin cans. That way we can phone each other from a long distance, but the thread is always breaking.

Our Uncle Phidyme pulled up in his machine and he said to our mother:

"Niece, today I'm borrowing your two fine, big lads and I'm taking them to Quebec. Your aunt, my wife, thinks I go to Quebec for fun. She doesn't know what it means to go to the city. Life's much harder than it is here. So I'd like to have your two fine lads to keep an eye on me in Quebec. Besides that, I'd be proud to teach them about the greatness of the world."

Our mother looked at us, at our oldest brother and me. When I saw how she was looking, I thought she'd say no. She said:

"Uncle Phidyme, wouldn't you rather take me to keep an eye on you in Quebec?"

Our oldest brother and I, we were insulted. Our mother was trying to take our place. She was practically saying that our oldest brother and I couldn't keep an eye on Uncle Phidyme. This was the first time I'd had a chance to go to Quebec. My tonsils didn't want to grow. When would I get another chance? I protested:

"We can keep an eye on our uncle."

"My dear children," said our Uncle Phidyme, "in this life, luck doesn't often come to call. Grab hold of it! Nowadays, what with the war and submarines and atomic bombs and earthquakes, we don't know how much longer Quebec will stay together."

Now our mother was looking at the machine. I had the feeling, just looking at her looking, that she was the one who was going away. Finally, she shrugged her shoulders and said:

"Very well, Uncle Phidyme, I know you'd much rather have the children keep an eye on you."

"My lovely niece, if I took you to Quebec with me, you know very well that all the gals in the village would be jealous."

"Uncle Phidyme, our children will go to Quebec and keep an eye on you if you promise you'll behave yourself like a man who doesn't need someone to keep an eye on him. I wouldn't want our children to see why it is you need watching."

"Niece, your children are going to see business and nothing but: pure business. . . . Youngsters, get in the machine!"

You know our uncle's machine, God. It's a car

from the olden days, from before when he was born, I think. It isn't modern like the modern machines today. It's long, almost like a locomotive. It has several horse powers. Quite a few horses could fit under the hood. Our aunt, Uncle Phidyme's wife, is always complaining about the machine because their eighteen children can't all fit in. There's only two seats. Luckily, behind the machine there's a "rumble seat." That's an English word our Uncle Phidyme learned in Quebec; it means a seat in the back of a car that you can open or shut like a trunk and it has a leather chair inside it. Do You know what I'm talking about, God? It's as if you opened up the trunk of the machine but inside, instead of a spare tire and a jack, there's a chair that folds or unfolds. That isn't modern.

Our Uncle Phidyme's in the habit of telling us:

"I'm interested in a thing if I discover it's been out of style for two or three generations: if it still lasts, that means it's modern."

Our brother and I climbed into the rumble seat. God, why do all the parts of the machine have English names? Who is it that's responsible for baptizing parts? It seems to me the machine would still work even if the names of the parts were in French.

It's so nice in that leather chair at the back of the car! You feel like guests. You're up higher, you can see farther, you get more wind in your face, and all you can see of Uncle Phidyme is the top of his head, which is hidden by his cap.

The air smelled of hay. We were sneezing because of the strong smell that came into our noses. When a smell touches your brain, you cough. Our hair was blowing in the wind. Uncle Phidyme was driving pretty fast. A lot faster, anyway, than the cows that were flopped in their pastures, chewing their cuds and lying on their milk-bags. Your cows look very dumb, God!

The sky was so beautiful. You didn't make anything more beautiful, God. I'm not surprised that You're up there. It's the most beautiful place. Myself, though, I'd like to stay on Earth a little longer. . . . Soon we could see mountains on the horizon: all these places I'd never seen and that I'd like to visit some day. Then came the river that runs along the road, and Mont Orignal, as steep as the muzzle of the moose it was named after. We weren't going fast, but on Mont Orignal the machine stirred up a cloud of dust: it was like fog that got caught in the big blue spruce trees.

God, You made my eyes too small for everything You created. It's impossible to look at it all. Along the road there were dandelions and daisies and raspberries on the fences; there were houses and stables and horses and clotheslines with all kinds of clothes hanging on them to dry in the wind. You had to look quickly because the machine was anxious to get to Quebec.

With all that wind in my eyes and ears and nose, I was almost asleep, as if I was dazed. It was kind of like a dream. We were moving along with our little cloud of dust behind us; we were climbing up and down the hills; we were following curves; we were driving through villages; we could see steeples in the distance with houses clustered around, like chicks around a hen. Then the countryside got flatter. We saw fields of barley and wheat. Your world is so beautiful, God! There wasn't one cloud, only sun. Your whole world was painted with that wonderful light. Our oldest brother and I were as happy in our back seat as princes on a throne. I'd never thought that going to Quebec could give us so much happiness.

Our friends don't go to Quebec. They stay in the village. They'll never go to Quebec unless they have tonsils or mumps. They don't budge from the village. They stay there with the trees and cows and flies and butterflies and fences.

Soon we catch sight of Quebec, rising behind the hills. In my dream I could already see the River, which people say is as broad as the sea. I've never seen the sea. Already, I was imagining the Château Frontenac, built on Cap Diamant which Jacques Cartier discovered in 1534 — a very big castle, as big, from what I've heard, as if all the houses in our village were piled on top of one another. Below the Château, in the River, I was already imagining the boats anchored there, big boats, much bigger than the rowboats that Americans tie to the backs of their big machines to go fishing or hunting wild ducks, boats to float across the seas of the world.

There's boats from every country, except Germany, who we're at war with — even boats with radar and guns and torpedoes. Then I imagined the boat we'd board to go across the River, without getting out of the car, staying right in our seats; we'd keep driving toward Quebec on the boat. It was going to be my first time to see a real live boat. It was going to be my first time to cross a big river. It was going to be the first time to see, with my own eyes, the great city of Quebec. This time it wouldn't be a picture. I was going to see old houses built at the time of the kings of France, all made of stones. I was going to see the thick walls around the city to protect Quebec against the English cannonballs. I was going to see the cliff that the English climbed up to surprise the French and take Quebec away from them. I was going to see Quebec City, with its feet in the water of the St Lawrence River and its head in the clouds of the North.

We realized we were getting close to Quebec. So then my oldest brother and I sat up straight on our back seat and prepared ourselves to see what we were going to see. We didn't want to be surprised. We were a little bit afraid that we would be.

We saw big signs with QUEBEC written on them, and an arrow. Our Uncle Phidyme had taken a wrong turn. All of a sudden we saw an arrow that was pointing towards BOAT. Our oldest brother, who knows more things than I do, said:

"The boat's white, all white except for the smoke, and it's black."

I was thinking about my first boat, which I was soon going to see.

And Uncle Phidyme, God, I think You made him a little tight. I don't mean tight like the men that can't walk straight when they drink too much cider, I mean tight like people that like to have money but don't like to spend it. Just as we saw the smoke rising above a wall of houses — it must be the smoke from our boat — Uncle Phidyme said:

"Children, it costs a fortune to take the boat. Your uncle's a poor man; the good Lord allows us to cheat a little."

So then he asked us to bend over and lie on the floor of the back seat. We obeyed. And after that he shut the seat. It was dark and hot in there, God, as if we were at the Devil's.

Our oldest brother explained to me when we were driving up the gangplank of the boat that our Uncle Phidyme was parking the machine, that the boat was pulling away from the wharf, that the boat was travelling across the water of the St Lawrence River, that we were approaching Quebec under the Château Frontenac.

Our oldest brother understands some things better than I do. He explained to me how, by hiding us in the back seat, Uncle Phidyme was saving at least ten cents. We kept quiet because the boat police could put us in jail because we'd hidden so we could cross to Quebec for free.

Then the car started up again. We could tell that our Uncle Phidyme was in a hurry to leave. All of a sudden the machine stopped and our Uncle Phidyme opened the cover of the back seat. And then I saw Quebec! Amen.

16

Prayer
of
Thanks

Our mother says that "children always exaggerate." And our father? Does our mother listen to him? It would take quite a few children to exaggerate as much as he does. Once he took me fishing. I was with him at the general store when he told them about our fish. I'd never seen that livestock! There wasn't enough water in the river for a fish like that to swim in. Even if there had been enough water, our father's fish was so big he'd have had to run and get help just to pull it onto the shore. When our father tells about what we saw together, the two of us, at the same time, in the same place, I feel, God, that You created me almost blind. What You *did* do, God, was give our father a really powerful tongue. Thank you, God.

If his tongue wasn't powerful enough to make

the farmers of Dorchester and Bellechasse believe that his products are the best of all the
products in the world, he wouldn't come back
from travelling with a wad of dollars in his
pockets. The farmers would buy products that
weren't as good as his, and the cows and calves
and sheep would die like flies during the winter,
choking and coughing to death and eaten alive
by worms and lice. You've made life dangerous
for farm animals, God, but fortunately You created our father's good products and You gave our
father a tongue that can sell his good products to
the farmers. So then the animals are well taken
care of, they're in good health, and our mother
can put good animal meat on the table, and
cream and potatoes and carrots and butter and
cheese, and lots of pies and often even fudge.
Thank you, God, for everything You give our
family, and especially for our father's tongue.

With all that, I've forgotten why I came to see
You today. Old people forget everything, too.
What will I be able to remember when I'm really
old, when I'm forty or fifty? I don't want to live

to be that old. It isn't worth the trouble of living if we forget everything.

Am I old now? When I was two days old, I was twice as old as when I was one day old. When I was one day old . . . I don't know how to count that: one day is how many times older than zero days old? The day when they sent me to school, I was how many times older than when I was one day old? Six years is six times three hundred and sixty-five days and a quarter. That makes . . . I can't do it, I haven't got paper and a pencil. You're going to have to wait for the answer, God; I'll be back. Six times three hundred and sixty-five days and a quarter plus . . . I forgot, some months are multiplied by thirty days and some by thirty-one. . . . And leap years. . . . How old will I be in the year 2000? Well, I'd better go now because I forgot what it was that I wanted to tell You.

The nun at school told us: "Children, when you think you have nothing to say to God, tell Him thank You. There's always a reason to thank God."

So, God, I want to say thank You. Thank You for meat and milk and vegetables. . . . Thank You for ending the war in the old countries. Thank You for keeping peace here in Canada. Thank You for sending more peace than anywhere else to the counties of Beauce, Dorchester, Bellechasse and even Frontenac, where my other grandparents live and they don't have a war there either. Thank You for our father's tongue that doesn't talk much at home because he gives it a rest after talking too much in other places. Thank You for my brothers and the little squaller who arrived a while ago. I'd rather not have them but then, if I didn't have them, it would be as if I wasn't there myself. So I'd rather have them. As far as our mother's concerned, thank You, God. You could have given me another one, but I think that would have been a mistake.

The nun at school told us that on the whole Earth there's only one man who can't make any mistakes: Your pope. I can't believe that. I bet you that if I told Your holy pope: "Monsieur Pope, how much is seventeen times nineteen plus sixteen and one-eighth minus two and three-quarters," even if he had a pencil and paper he could make a mistake.

166
Roch
Carrier

Even if I took away the eighths and the quarters, he could make an error. If Your pope can't make an error, it would have been unfair for the other children when he was going to school. He would have always had the right answer and he'd have been the nun's teacher's pet. But I know that You're fair, God, and I know that You've given everybody the right to make errors. Even You, You like to make mistakes. What about measles? Don't tell me that wasn't a mistake. And Ginette, in our class, who was our age and died, don't tell me that wasn't a mistake. And I think You made a mistake when You forgot to give us wings like You gave the birds. Thank You, even if we don't have wings. It's better to be on Earth without wings than to not be here, even with wings.

Thank You again for our mother. Even if You wanted to give me a brand-new one, made to measure, I'd still rather keep our mother, though she's pretty worn-out. And thank You for our grandparents. Thank You for our grandfather, because he teaches me about fire, iron, wood, and hunting and fishing and his old dead father's secrets. Thank You, God, even if he teases me because of all the secrets about life and women that I don't know yet. Thank You for our grandmother who knows all the old songs and who has old legs that remember the dances from when she was a young girl. My friends and I, when we don't have anything to do, we go and see our grandmother and she gives us candy and she sings old songs that my friends' grandmothers have forgotten. Our grandmother crams our pockets full of candies and she tells the others: "Keep those candies and eat them under your grandmothers' noses so they'll learn not to be so tight-fisted with you." She enjoys it so much, she thinks all my friends are her grandsons, too. I don't like that very much myself, but I'm proud that they like our grandmother better than their grumpy old tight-wad stingy old grandmothers with rheumatism. Thank You God, and excuse me because I have to go outside and pee.